# BERLIN

# POetry

# CLUB

## Volume 1

By

# D.I. Jolly

www.dijolly.com

Printed and Published by

TinPot Publishing

**Berlin Poetry Club Volume One**

**Published by Tinpot Publishing**

Copyright of text and characters © D. I. Jolly

Except: The Great Gatsby by F. Scott Fitzgerald © Frances Scott Fitzgerald Lanahan.

Back Cover Photograph by Ted Titus

www.tinpotbooks.com                    First edition 2019                    ISBN:9781686360718

# Warning:

This book contains

Graphic and Adult themes.

All works presented here

are fictional.

# Prologue

The Berlin Poetry Club meets once a week to discuss and present their previous meeting's topic. The name is actually a joke as its' members are all short story writers.

Each of the stories in this anthology is a Poetry Club story; the titles are taken from the topic of that particular week. If you see stories with the same title, that's because more than one story was written in that time.

I hope you enjoy.

# Contents:

# Alone in the Dark

Dennis sat with his head on the kitchen table wondering if today would be the day he snapped and flips it over. A bright light shocked him into sitting up and he looked through bloodshot eyes at his wife, whose face turned sad.

"It really scares me when you sit in the dark like that."

"I'm sorry my love, I... I don't mean to bring this back into the house with me. I just wish I could find something else and leave this shit job once and for all."

Emily walked over to sat on his lap and lay her head on his shoulder.

"I know, I know, and you will. I'm sorry it's so hard for you right now, but I still love you."

He wrapped his arms around her and for an instant remembered why he got up day after day. She made his life make sense and as long as they were together, nothing else mattered. A smile crept back to his face.

"Let's open a bottle of wine, light a fire and lose track of time. I'm going to call in sick tomorrow."

"Really? You never do that, even when you are sick."

"Exactly. I'm 30 years old, not dead, let's have a holiday day."

"Oh... Uummm, ok, let's do it."

She jumped up off him and went to the cupboard for glasses. He headed into the lounge, pulled the cushions off the couch and started on a fire. A few hours and a bottle of wine each later, they stared into the fire quietly together.

A sudden and loud knock at the door broke the spell and Dennis looked at the clock.

"Who would be knocking at this hour?"

Emily shrugged as he got up and headed for the door which burst inwards as he got there. It knocked his head hard and he staggered backwards and to the ground. Through suddenly blurry eyes he saw three men rush into the house. He wanted to move to stop them but in that instant, his body wouldn't respond. A rough hand grabbed him and pulled him to his feet, then shoved him across the room. Emily came into focus and his mind cleared suddenly. He regained his balance and put himself between them and her.

"What the fuck do you want? Get out of my house!"

One of the men pointed his gun at Dennis and growled,

"Shut up. "

While the other two pulled the couch in front of the door. Fear and rage started to bubble up inside of Dennis, bringing with it an urge to do something stupid, but Emily's hands on his back kept him sane.

"What do you want?"

The man stepped forward and put the gun against Dennis's forehead.

"Shut, up... and sit down."

As he spoke he put his spare hand on Dennis's shoulder and pushed him hard, causing him to stumble. In his ear, he heard a whisper.

"Let's just do as they say."

Slowly he and Emily sat down quietly. The other two men appeared and they all started talking amongst themselves. Dennis strained his ear to try and hear what they were saying but couldn't make any of it out, but did notice one of them constantly looking Emily up and down. A growing sense of desperation to get these men out of his house and away from his wife had started creeping through his mind, and it made his arms start to shake. Suddenly the three men erupted into an argument, all their focus turned to each other, and Dennis's mind was instantly calm. He turned to look at Emily, kissed her hands and mentally said goodbye.

In one swift motion, he turned back towards the men, stood up and grabbed an empty wine bottle, all set to start the fight of his life. He moved faster than he could ever have imagined and smashed the bottled over the head of the man with the gun while throwing his shoulder against one of the others. He had to win; no part of him was willing to accept any other possibility and it made his hits harder, his reactions fast and his tolerance for pain higher. It wasn't a perfect Hollywood fight, it was raw and brutal. Dennis could feel that he was bleeding and his one eye was swelling shut and that his jaw was probably broken, but the others were worse. The first man hadn't recovered from the broken bottle and in a final spectacular motion Dennis ducked under a wild swing, grabbed a chair and smashed it across one of their faces. He turned his ferocity towards the last man standing who had already managed to get the front door open and was halfway down the street.

Dennis stared at the carnage of his home, blood, broken furniture, glass and bodies. But he'd won, he had defeated the invaders and Emily was going to be alright. The calm that came with the thought also stripped him of his adrenaline and exhaustion suddenly gripped every fibre of his being. He staggered towards his wife feeling sanity slip away with every movement. He could feel his consciousness fading but had to see her, had to make sure she was alright. She stared at him, broken, but standing and could hardly believe what she'd witnessed. Her tear-filled smile gave him just enough hope to reach out a shaky hand and stroke her cheek.

*

A white flash filled Dennis's vision blinding him for a second and he fell backwards onto the padded floor of his room.

"Hey, what are you doing?'

The nurse looked confused at the apparent anger on the doctor's face.

"Why were the lights' out in his room?"

"He looked like he was trying to sleep and it's always so bright in there, I thought it would help."

The doctor shook her head.

"You can't do that with this one, when he's alone in the dark he relieves the day of his breakdown over and over again."

"What? How?"

"He has been here for almost 3 years. 3 years ago some men broke into his house and tried to hold him and his wife hostage. He snapped and attacked them, trying to drive them out."

"Oh my god, so the three men beat him into this state?"

The doctor smiled again a little sadly.

"No, he actually managed to superhero the situation. He was battered but he took them down."

"So what happened?"

"At the last minute just before the police arrived one of the home invaders pulled a gun and shot him in the back..."

The doctor sighed and looked back at the monitors, at Dennis curled up in the corner of his room.

"...The bullet passed right through him and hit his wife in the head. At the last second everything he'd fought for died in front of him. In that moment he just ...broke! Only to have him relive the whole experience every night. It took us weeks to work out what was going on when he first got here. Now we just know to always leave the lights on."

The nurse bit her bottom lip and turned to also look at him as he reached out a shaking hand and gently wiped the tear from his wife's cheek before closing his eyes to cry.

# Precious Gift

I have something for you, something I didn't realise I had taken from you, or … maybe you gave it to me, I can't tell. I'm going to give you your life back. How? You ask.  Simply by taking myself out of it. Somewhere on this road we've been walking you got lost and neither of us noticed. I know this might seem cruel and I know you will probably hate me. Maybe just at first or maybe forever, but that's ok. I can handle that. The really bad news is that I can't just give your life back; you also have to be willing to take it back. The only thing I know is that, I don't love you anymore. If I'm honest I'm not sure that I ever did, and I think you know that on some level. I think... I think that's why you changed so much over our time together. You've been trying to turn yourself into the person I could love and in so doing just stopped being you.

I do also want to say that I'm sorry. I'm sorry I didn't realise it sooner, I'm sorry there isn't a better or different way to handle this problem. I'm sorry that after everything you've done and put yourself through for me, in the end, you're still the one who's getting hurt. And finally, I'm sorry that I'm not doing this in person. To continue down the path of brutal honesty it's not because I'm not strong enough but because I don't think you would have been. Which is one of the things that's changed since we first met. I hope, actually that by pointing that out you'll realise that it's true and it'll help to encourage you to go back to living your life in a way that is better for you.

I know your friends miss you, because, I miss you. The you that I met those years ago. We might not have ever been made for *each other but we used to be much closer then, than we are now. Do not look for me, do not try and contact me, don't call my family, my friends. Give up on me and forget about us, go, please, and focus on yourself. There is a better version of you out there and a better match for you. Really for the last year all we've done is waste each other's time and I think we both deserve better than that.*

*Merry Christmas.*

Richard turned the letter over in his hands a few times as his mind began fighting the truth in front of him, the small ring box in his pocket suddenly feeling like it weighed a ton, and pulled him to the ground. After a few long moments he blinked the tears out of his eyes and read the letter again, waiting for the joke to end, for the big reveal, for his girlfriend to jump out of one of the boxes and yell surprise. But it never happened, and eventually he had to admit to himself that she wasn't his girlfriend, but his ex. Slowly he picked himself up off the floor and tried to start his day. His morning shower lasted longer than usual and he dropped his first mug filled with coffee, which made him jump and yell, which made him start crying. But, he pulled himself together and cleaned up the mess and tried again. He spent a long time deciding whether or not he was going to go to his friends Christmas party as planned and in the end decided he needed to. He knew he would be the life and soul-destroyer of the party but that if they were his friends it would be alright. It wasn't a big party and maybe he needed to do something for himself. To get back to a version of himself that people could recognise again. Perhaps that started by being a little selfish, or maybe it was asking for help, he couldn't tell. When he arrived he just handed his host the letter and stood waiting for their reaction and when they wrapped their arms around him he started to cry, again. But it felt different to the first few times, at home alone it was a hopeless cry, this felt more like a release, a let go cry, and as he did so a small voice in the back of his mind started to think very quietly that maybe, just maybe, the letter was right about him, and that she had given him his life back.

# Let's Play

"If life is just God and the devil playing chess, and we're all pawns, then who are the other pieces?"

"What do you mean?"

"Well, only half the pieces on a chess board are pawns. So, who are the king and queen, who are the knights, the bishops and the castles?"

"Uummmm, I think you're taking this metaphor a bit too seriously."

"Am I? Or are you not taking it seriously enough. I mean, in chess if you get a pawn across the board it can become a different more powerful piece. Maybe that's a way of saying it's possible to become more than what you started as. What if those pieces are the innovators, the drivers of industry and change? Da Vinci could have been a Knight thinking in new and different directions. Dr King and Gandhi, bishops driving the world to change. Justinian a King in the true sense, leading people into a new world."

"Wait, who?"

"A Roman emperor, amazing man, had the Hagia Sophia built. Changed the world through personal drive."

The table fell into a comfortable silence as both men thought about it, looking at the old metaphor through new eyes. After a while his friend broke the silence.

"I think the thing that bothers me most about this idea isn't that it implies the existence of God and the devil, it's that for a game to truly have meaning someone has to be able to win. And if you factor in God and the devil, and the original confrontation where Lucifer announced that he was more powerful than God, then, if he could win, that, that would prove him right and God wrong."

"Well, unless this is just the test, Lucifer announces his belief in himself; God challenges him to a chess game to see if he's right."

Silence hit them again but this time it seemed to bring a coldness with it.

"But that would mean, that all of existence as we know it, all life as we know it really is a just chess game and … that it doesn't matter who wins because once the game is over… it's all over."

Another cold shiver hit them both and they looked away from each other, suddenly feeling uneasy and unsure of their place in the universe. Time slipped by as they sat motionless, both desperately trying not to think, then suddenly he rose, walked across the room and started setting up an old chessboard his grandfather had given him.

"What are you doing?"

"The way I figure it is, as long as a chess game is being played then the chess game can't be over and that will at least give us that much time."

"That's ridiculous!"

"Yes, yes it is."

He smiled at his friend who stared at him for a moment, then smiled himself.

"Shall we get a drink after this?"

"I think I'd like that."

# Wet

Michal opened his eyes and stared for a moment at the wall. 'Kill or be killed' painted on every spare piece of wall and ceiling across his cell. He sighed, climbed out of bed staggering to the toilet in the corner to start his morning rituals. As he sat there he scratched a little mark into the wall. It had been just over two years since he'd been taken. That day walking home from school in the pouring rain, soaked through and freezing, desperate to just get home and get warm. So desperate in fact that he hadn't noticed the van following him until it pulled up alongside him and he was pulled inside.

Every day since then he'd spent at the camp, some rich psychopath's idea of fun. Kidnapped children and young teens forced to train and forced to fight. Kill or be killed. Every now and then some new combatants would refuse, their shock collars would go off and they'd be hung by the neck above the arena, as a reminder to everyone else. If you don't fight, you all die. Michal stepped into the shower and closed his eyes as the water ran over him, trying to imagine he was still just walking home in the rain.

Each cell was self-contained, the Psycho didn't let the kids see or talk to each other outside the arena, for fear of an uprising. There was a bang at his cell door and the sound of a tray sliding against concrete. It was Fight Day, which meant no training and better food. He had a knack for fighting and had managed to survive a lot longer than anyone else. A rumour had started that he couldn't be beaten and so the announcers started calling him

The Demon, and he'd started having to fight more than one kid at once. Tonight he had to fight four in a weapons match and wasn't looking forward to it. A part of him just thought about giving up, letting the other kids win and just letting it be over. But he always thought that the morning of a fight, and when he stepped into the arena and saw the Psycho sitting on his throne looking down at them, he just couldn't do it. He had to survive; he couldn't let that bastard break him. So he fought and he won and went back to his cell and let the cycle continued. With each win, he got a little bit more wriggle room. It had started simply with a mattress, then a blanket. A bit more food here and bit more hot water there. Eventually, he got to keep his favourite weapons and his armour, with his own modifications, so it fitted him better. Every show of loyalty brought him one step closer to the man himself and once he got close enough he would rip out his heart with his bare hands.

The fight ended quickly, three of kids were already so scared of him that it didn't seem fair. He'd seen them fight with much more skill in the past but when they were up against him it was different. One of them held his nerve though and actually did himself proud, but not proud enough. With a quick flick of his sword, the point opened the boys main vain and warm blood erupted like a fountain, covering Michal and even reaching as high as the Psycho, who stood up and clapped his approval. Michal bowed graciously and then stood patiently waiting for the doors to open so he could just return to his cell.

"Well Done Michal, you are the most skilled fighter I have ever had come through here and I'm so proud of you."

Michal looked up in shock; he'd never heard the Psycho speak before.

"Th...Thank you."

He croaked.

"So I have a special reward for you, it's waiting back in your cell. I hope you like it and we will see you tomorrow because you will be fighting every day this week."

Michal eyebrows raised, the Psycho wasn't nice or kind and everything he said sent a cold shiver down his spine. The doors opened and he was led back to his cell. There lying on his bed was his 'reward.' She looked in her mid to late 20s, a bit too thin and pale to be healthy, but had a pretty face.

"You must be The Demon."

Her voice was shaky and her eyes kept tracing down his body reminding him that he was covered in blood.

"I'm your reward."

She stood up and let her dress slip to the floor, leaving her totally naked. At 14 when he'd been taken, girls were still a mystery, and 2 years in death camp had offered no extra insight. But he knew that as much as his body pushed towards her, it was wrong. He closed his eyes and turned his head away.

"I... I... you, we don't have to do this."

"You don't like what you see?"

She stepped up closer to him and ran a hand down his face.

"You can look, I don't mind, I like it."

Michal opened his eyes again but forced himself to look into her face.

"I need to shower."

"Oh, now we're getting somewhere."

She let her hands start trying to undo his amour but he caught her by the wrist.

"I'm not doing this."

Fear crept into her eyes.

"If you don't, they'll kill me. Please, I-I don't want to die."

He stared at her for a long minute and watched as the tears welled up and then slowly began running down her face. He let her go and then whispered.

"Ok… ok, ok, but uummm… But I've never done this before."

She forced a smile.

"That's ok honey, I'll show you."

She helped him remove his armour and the rest of his clothes before they stepped into the shower. She couldn't help but stare at the scars that cover over half his body, and he tried not to notice as he washed the blood out of his hair. Still dropping from the shower she led him back to the bed and took his virginity.

In the morning when he opened his eyes and read the walls again he wondered if it wasn't just a dream.

# Dolls

Michal slipped back into his usual morning routine but couldn't help but feeling off, flatter than usual and wondered if what was left of his spirit had finally given up.

When he stood outside the arena the doors waiting for them to open, he thought again about giving up and letting them kill him and letting it be over. Then his mind went to the girl, and how desperate she had looked when she thought he would resist. He wondered where she was kept normally. She didn't look like she was forced to train like the fighters. The doors to the arena opened, and for the first few seconds, Michal found himself distracted and unfocused. Then the first hit landed, knocking him off his feet and back to his senses.

No weapons this time, hand to hand with two other boys, both larger than him but also both new. Having landed a solid hit gave them both a bit of confidence, but it didn't change the outcome. Once Michal had managed to break the neck of the boy who'd hit him, the courage left the other and the fight ended quickly. As usual, in the end, he turned to face the Psycho and bowed.

"Interesting, did yesterday's reward distract you perhaps? I hope not, it's waiting for you again. This time though, try and enjoy it. It's your new toy; it's your plaything to do with what you will. I want you to have fun with it."

It... Thing... Toy... The words send a bolt of red-hot rage through Michal's mind, but he contained himself. He bowed and thanked his captor. He was then led back to his room where she was waiting for him. Once again she helped him wash out the blood before they returned to his bed, and all without speaking. When they'd finished and simply lay together Michal realised that being with her was the first none violent contact he'd had since being taken. She lay in his arms and together they felt safe there.

In the morning he woke and read the walls again and fought to forget that feeling. At the start of the next fight, he first had to battle himself and get his mind on what he was doing before he could focus the other boys. The rest of the week continued the same way until the end of the fifth fight. He had once again won, but once again had taken a few blows that he would normally have been able to avoid. He turned and bowed at the Psycho.

"Michal my boy, this has been an interesting week, watching you has become fun again and I like it. So tomorrow we will up the stakes. Tonight your toy will not be waiting for you, but tomorrow it will be here to watch you. So get some sleep."

His room felt empty without her and a cold loneliness had crept in. He found it hard to fall asleep without her there and woke up feeling strange, angrier than he'd expected, and nervous. As he showered he thought about her watching him fight. Would she be excited? Would she be horrified? Would she feel anything? Which was better? These questions continued to circle his mind until he stepped into the arena. He took a moment and scanned the seating area for his reward until he saw her. Hanging above the arena floor, strung up like a marionette doll with her eyes forced open staring down at him. Suddenly the other doors opened and instead of boys, guards marched in, all armed and smiling.

# Gates to Another World

Michal's shoulders dropped and he turned his attention back to the woman hanging over him. For a few seconds, he desperately tried to work out if she was still alive. He searched her face hoping to find some twitch, some movement, anything. Then all at once the top of her head exploded out showering him in brain and blood. He levelled his gaze and stared at the guards, one of whom was holding a gun.

"Oh I'm sorry, did I break your toy?"

The guards erupted in maniacal laughter and a cold shiver ran down Michal's body. His mind cleared, and all the distracting thought that had been building over the week vanished. The muscles in his shoulders tightened; he took a deep breath.

"I am the Demon, hunter of men."

And he swung his sword down hard at his own neck. The blade sliced through the lock of his shock collar, but only lightly grazed his actual neck. The laughter stopped as the guards watched the collar fall to the ground and before they could look up Michal was on them. Only one managed to get a single shot off before they all died, and it hit the wall. Michal didn't stop to see if the Psycho had waited for the results of the fight, and ran through the open gate into the labyrinth of tunnels that was The Camp. He moved with speed and purpose towards where he believed he could find the throne room, stopping only for a moment at a small control panel to unlock all the doors across the camp.

The tunnels began to fill with the sound of running and shouting boys, and then fighting and gunshots as the guards tried in vain to stop them. Michal, however, hadn't waited around and was back on the hunt. After a few left and right turns he found himself standing in front of a doorway and it stopped him dead. There on the other side shining back at him was sunlight, the first he'd seen in over two years. There was grass and trees and as he took a few nervous steps closer he could even see the sky.

The doorway seemed to shine and an idea long locked away came back to him and he whispered,

"Freedom."

He'd spent so much time focusing on killing the Psycho that he'd forgotten about the idea of escaping. And now here it was in front of him. Like a gateway into another world, a world of light where he wouldn't have to fight or kill anyone anymore. He could even try finding his family. Tears welled up in his eyes as he remembered vaguely that he wanted to be an artist when he grew up, and draw comic books. Slowly he stepped forward through the doorway and had to cover his eyes to shield them from the light, so didn't see who struck him hard on the side of the face. He fell to the ground and frantically started blinking to get his vision back as a barrage of brutal kicks came from seemingly everywhere. Through the blur, he managed to grab hold of the leg and rolled pulling his attacker to the ground.

"You've ruined everything! Years of work! Do you know how long I've spent building this empire?"

The voice was familiar and as his vision cleared the Psycho came into view. Michal quickly rolled away and got to his feet to face him properly.

"I'm going to enjoy killing you boy!" Spat the Psycho furiously as he charged at Michal who dodged out the way catching him by the arm and breaking it effortlessly. The thought of finally exacting his desired revenge flashed in his mind but he let go and let the man drop to the floor. They stared at each other for a few seconds in silence and the man slowly got to his feet.

"What are you waiting for then, go on! Kill me, Demon."

Michal let his mind fall back to the wonder he'd felt when he saw the light and the sky.

"I don't want to kill you. I don't want to kill anyone."

He reached down and picked up his sword which he'd dropped and slipped it into his belt.

"But if I ever see you again, but then, I don't think I have to worry about that."

Michal pointed back at the doorway where all the other children had started to gather. Then he turned and ran off into the light to go and find his new life in this strange new, old world.

# Consciousness of Death

*"After finishing The Camp story line, the character of Michal has come up again and will continue to appear in stories occasionally when it makes sense. This is the rest of his story so far."*

Violence has a way of staining a soul. It doesn't matter how you interacted with it, once it's there, it's there. And those who know can see it.

After leaving The Camp Michal managed to find his way back to his country, his family and his home. He didn't hide what had happened, but never spoke about it in detail, and his family were more than thrilled to see him trying to live a normal life. But violence was never far away. After returning to school it was only two weeks before his parents were called to the headmaster's office. The three main bullies of the school had been antagonising him since his return, trying to prove themselves against him. Rumours of where he'd been and what he'd done, had spread like wildfire. On that particular day, they surrounded him and started throwing more than words. After the third time, one of them had punched him, witnesses said there was a shift in the way Michal stood and he said simply.

"I will not let you do that again."

The bullies laugh, moved forward and before anyone could comprehend what had happened Michal had all but killed all three boys. This was backed up by over a dozen videos of the incident. This also showed him performing aftercare to one of the boys which eventually saved his life. Michal did not apologise, and was told to take more time to adjust before returning to school. Struggling to know what to do, his parents took him to visit his grandfather in a care home. From the moment they walked into the visitor's lounge he noticed two women sitting in the corner watching him. Their conversation had abruptly stopped and they stared. Off in another corner a man also turned to focus on him. His grandfather, the man he was named after however, was overjoyed and wrapped his arms around him, kissed his cheeks and cried. They sat together for over an hour while his grandfather spoke at length about everything that he'd missed and how much he was missed. Until Michal excused himself, rose and went to the older man sitting alone. He sat down in front of him and for a minute they simply watched each other.

"You bring death with you, boy. I could see it the moment you arrived. You are too young to be a veteran though."

"Is that what you are? Is that what they are?"

He gestured with his head towards the women.

"Yes. In the war. I was a forward scout turned sniper, I was... Successful. They, on the other hand, were nurses."

Michal turned and looked at them for a moment.

"I wonder who has the most blood on their hands."

After another long quiet minute, the man let his face turn grave.

"I believe, you do."

"Four... hundred, and twenty-seven."

"Did you know any of their names?"

"Sixteen."

"You still know their names."

Michal recognised that he wasn't being asked a question so gestured towards the man in reply.

"Only 91 and 7 names. William, Robert, Morgan, Frank, George, Stacy and Rebecca."

"In that order?"

"In that order."

"Why do you say I bring death with me?"

"Because I can see him. Standing over your shoulder, like he used to stand over mine. Guiding your hands like he used to guide my bullets. Probably thinks it's easier to stay near you, rather than go looking for souls himself. *They* can see him too, spent so long trying to ward him off I can't imagine they appreciate you just bringing him in here like that."

Michal lowered his head slightly and looked over his shoulder. Not sure if he was looking at the women or the lingering shadow they all saw.

"Does it get easier?"

"The burden? The knowledge of what you've done and what you know you can do?"

"No, the pretending."

"With practise, but you'll never fool yourself."

Michal rose silently and went back to his family. Brushed off the whole thing as someone he'd once met and  wanted to talk to, and then spent the rest of the day pretending to smile. That night the old man died and in the morning, Michal returned to school.

# Speak of the Devil

Ben and Thomas quietly sipped their drinks and waited for comfort to set in. Although their lives had taken very different paths after escaping The Camp, nothing would stop them from coming to their yearly meet up. There were three-years between them, which meant almost nothing as they were now in their late 20's, but it had meant the world when they were kidnapped at ages 7 and 10. They had been transported together and Thomas had instantly taken to trying to protect Ben as best he could. They were some of the lucky ones who arrived only a few weeks before the breakout, and neither of them had to fight. But they had been forced to see the type of things that never truly went away.

After the second beer was done and Thomas returned with a third, he had found his words.

"How's it going at the new job?"

"Yeah, not bad. I get Thursday and Saturdays off and they pay for my travel card which pretty is cool."

"That's good, you able to save anything?"

Ben took a thirsty sip of his beer.

"A little, not every week, but at least once a month."

"You still living at the same place?"

Ben blushed now and looked down.

"No, no. I… I had to move out. Well, no I didn't have to but I, kind thought I oughta."

Thomas nodded knowingly and sighed.

"You started having nightmares again."

It wasn't a question and they both knew it.

"I… I couldn't shift my sessions to my day off, and so I ran out of the pills. But, but that's all sorted now and I didn't just spend the money you sent, I-I kept it."

He reached into his pocket and pulled out a small envelope which he handed to Thomas. It was full of cash and it filled Thomas's heart with a deep and guilty pride. He wanted to just hand it back, almost as a reward for doing the right thing but he couldn't be sure if that wouldn't just wound the guy. He knew he was struggling and to just keep the money aside and give it back when it was probably more than he'd made that month. It showed heart, it reminded Thomas of why he was so dedicated to helping. He pocketed the envelope and said.

"Same dream as always?"

Ben took another long sip of his beer and thought, letting his gaze grow distant.

"You know it's funny, of everything, the guys with the whips on the boat, The Camp guards, the guy in charge, the trainers. The only thing that still comes to me in the night … is him. Everything else faded but he's still …"

Ben's lip started shaking and he closed his eyes against the welling tears.

"And he's the guy who ended up saving us. Fuck."

Ben ran a shaking hand over his face, and a cold shiver ran over Thomas's body as he too thought back to that time.

"The Demon Hunter of Men … Michal."

Thomas's voice dropped to a whisper.

"The Devil."

They both raised their glasses.

"I hope he found peace where ever he is, and I pray that it's far away from here."

Michal smiled as he heard the words from his perch at the bar, he'd tuned into the conversation when he heard the word nightmares. He wouldn't have been able to pick them out as kids from The Camp any more than they knew what he actually looked like, but it made him smile and a bit sad when he stumbled across the others. The ones who had been there with him and had managed to get back to the real world. Quietly he raised his own glass and thought, 'and to you'. He took a sip, paid his tab and walked out. Careful not to glace across and see their faces. He didn't need to know who they were but was glad to know others were out there, looking after for each other. Besides, what good would meeting The Devil in a bar do anyway?

# Forever

Barbara bit down hard on her bottom lip, trying to stop her tears. Knowing full well it wasn't going to work. While Rick just sat there, staring at her across the table.

"Look, I'm sorry I'm hurting you, but I just... I'm just not that guy, I... I don't have the feeling you're hoping for."

"How would you know? You're not even willing to try. We have so much fun together, we like all the same things. We don't even have sex every night but still sleep together and now you think we can just be friends! What's wrong with you?"

Her voice was sharp with no attempt to hide her pain. Rick's heart was beating so hard in his chest you could see his shirt move. His mind split into two voices. One lying, telling him that it was better to do it now to save her greater heartbreak later, the other told the truth and called him a coward, said he knew exactly how she'd felt, and how he felt and that he was simply running away.

"I don't know what else to say."

The tears were running freely down her face, as he got up and headed for the door. She wanted to run after him and beg him to just try, tell him she'd be there with him and it wasn't as scary to fall in love as he thought. But she was so angry and so hurt that all she could do was sit there and cry. Then all at once, she knew exactly what she was going to do, she knew exactly how she could get her message across to him, and in a way that he wouldn't be able to deny or ignore. She looked into herself, gathered up the shattered pieces of her heart, paid for the coffee and left.

Rick continued to berate himself all the way to his favourite bar where his friends were waiting. He'd managed to spin the story that she came across as irrational and unstable, and they'd all been joking about him ending up in her basement. It was funny during the day but as the night had set in he'd started to lose his sense of humour. He wasn't about to admit that to his friends though. In his mind, that would mean that he did actually have feelings for her, and it was far too soon for that thought.

"So how did it go?"

"Well, I didn't die so that's a win. Shame though, poor girl, oh well... Next!"

"Ha, nice!"

"Yeah man, she was nuts it's better for all of us now that that's over."

*

As the night went on Rick managed to drink and flirt his way past his feelings and into a fun night out. Meanwhile, Barbara taped a letter to his front door, and let herself in.

*

Rick put his arm around a girl whose name he couldn't remember and smiled as he tried to tell himself that this made much more sense than getting into a relationship. He glanced at his friends who nodded in approval and slight envy. Which he both loved and hated. Suddenly the voices in his head started to wonder if he sacrificed relationships just to remain 'cool' in the eyes of his drinking buddies and, what the fuck he was actually doing with his life. He often joked about dying alone but happy in the bed of a pretty girl but had always hoped it was just a joke. Now it suddenly felt too real. He looked at the girl and saw another broken heart he'd tell his friends was crazy and it sobered him up. Barbara's words rushed back to his mind causing him to physically shudder.

"Hey, honey what's wrong? You don't look so well?"

"Me? Yeah, I'm fiiiiine."

"Yes, you are."

Rick looked at her and wondered what kind of arsehole he really was, and what kind he wanted to be. He let his eyes run over the girl and realised he was physically capable. 'Kiss her, then fuck her. Everything will be fine in the morning.' The standard plan. He downed the rest of his beer and started making out with her, but it still didn't seem like a good idea. So he had a shot and tried again. Barbara again appeared in his mind and again he physically recoiled, as if he could pull his head away from the memory.

"Fuck it I'm going home."

"What? Man, what's going on?"

"I don't know, I'm just... tired, and too in my head, sorry I've got to go home I'll call you tomorrow."

Without another word he grabbed his jacket and left, leaving the nameless girl sitting on the couch, wondering what she'd done wrong. Rick was the dangerous combination of smart, charming and handsome, and knew how to use it to his advantage. As he walked home he started to hate himself for not saying goodbye to the girl he'd been making out with, on top of thinking about how Barbara had looked when he'd just left her in the coffee shop.

He stopped and stared for a minute at the envelope on his door before taking it down. He knew who it was from; she wasn't the first woman to write him a letter. He always hated reading them and really, really didn't want to deal with one now, but decided it would be better to just get it out of the way. He sat with his back against the door and started reading.

*Rick. I don't know what I did that made you run away so fast. I want to be sorry but I'm not sure I actually did anything wrong. I thought we were on a path together and apparently, we weren't, but until you turned and ran away you hadn't given me any clues to that's how you felt and that's a dangerous way to play with a woman's heart. But, I guess, that's also who you are and it would be equally short-sighted of me to hope you could just be different for my sake. You said you wanted to be friends but we both know that's just what someone says, we're not going to be friends. I don't hate you but that's not the same as I forgive you. But I have a present for you. I've put it inside along with your key...*

Rick rolled his eyes and blinked a few times,

"God damn this letter I might be too drunk for this."

He turned the page over in his hands to see how much there still was to read and decided to just finish it.

*...I do want you to be better though, for your sake, not mine. If you let fear like this continue to drive your actions then you are*

*going to end up alone and you're much too nice a guy to end up like that. So I hope my little gift will act as a reminder to you to open up your heart and take a risk on people. I don't mean fall in love with the first person who comes along, but next time, when you say you're open to the idea, to really honestly mean it, and not just say it because it's the correct answer.*

*I don't know if I loved you yet, but I really was open to the idea.*

*Goodbye.*

*Barbara.*

He sighed again feeling even more like an arsehole, but also cringed at the thought of a present, hoping it wasn't some cliché teddy bear, or god awful piece of art he'd have to hide or deal with. He opened his door and there she was waiting for him, totally naked, hanging from the back of his bedroom door. The world stopped spinning as he stared at her, rejecting the reality in front of him. It wasn't true, it wasn't happening, it was a nightmare. He waited a few moments longer to wake up. Then as suddenly as it had stopped the world shatter. He ran forward towards her, unhooked her from the door, tears streaming from his eyes.

"No, no nono no NO! Please fuck God no!"

He stupidly put his fingers against her neck hoping he could feel something or that it might help. Her head fell back and saw the words 'remember me' written on her forehead in lipstick. Her face was blue and her eyes milky. He stared at her for a few seconds frozen by fear then quickly crawled away to vomit into a flower pot.

"No, we joked that you were crazy, you weren't crazy, it was me, not you…"

He looked back at her and a shiver erupted from the base of his neck sending goose bumps over his whole body, turning it numb. He reached into his pocket to pull out his phone to call an ambulance, then opened a bottle of wine and sat down next to her drinking from it, waiting for them to arrive. Forcing himself to study her face. He never wanted to forget it. It had all started when she'd admitted that after spending two weeks almost constantly together she was really started to fall for him, and he let the fear push away someone who he actually liked, and he was never going to forget her, never let himself forget her. He would never love anyone the way he loved her.

# Unicorns

"Once upon a time, here on earth, there lived a beautiful and magical race of creatures. Horse-like in appearance, but stronger and with a single horn coming from their foreheads, the Unicorns were the manifestation of compassion and love."

"But mommy, if Unicorns were on earth why aren't they here now?"

The little girl's face showed a moment of genuine sadness, suddenly desperate for Unicorns to be real.

"Well, many, many years ago the evil King Rufus was envious of the Unicorn's power and beauty and wanted to take it for himself. He was a wicked man who had never known love or compassion and hated them for this. So, in a dark moment, he allied himself with the Black Dragons. Where Unicorns were light, they were darkness, hatred and fury, and King Rufus went to war. Which made the Unicorns very sad, they didn't want war with anyone or anything, but they also knew that they couldn't simply let love be driven out of the world. Where Dragons were strong, Unicorns were wise, and they came together in secret and combined their magic, sending a ray of pure love into the heart of King Rufus. That moment of love was all it took to change him forever, and he suddenly realised what damage he was doing and how the world needed Unicorns and love to exist. But many Unicorns had been lost in the war and those that were left were very weak after sending their love to the king. So, the last of them came together again, and turned themselves into sunlight then sent their beautiful rays of love into the hearts of all the children around the world."

"Woooooow"

"So you see sweetheart, Unicorns do still exist, they live as a little ray of sunlight in your heart, and as long as you stay kind and compassionate and good, they will continue to live on forever."

The little girl looked down at her heart and smiled, then hugged her mom goodnight and rolled over to sleep, happy knowing that the unicorn in her heart would be watching over her.

# Pumpkin

Johnny sat on his couch, patiently eating his cereal and waiting for his flatmate to wake up. It was almost four in the afternoon so he was sure he wouldn't have to wait too much longer. Josh walked sleepily into the kitchen to pour himself some coffee then went to join him on the couch.

"Morning man."

"Morning."

Johnny's voice was flat and he stared at Josh until he began to get uncomfortable.

"What?"

Johnny pointed,

"Care to explain why our coffee table is full of giant pumpkin?"

Josh suddenly sprung to life,

"Oh my God that's right, last night man, last night was the most amazing night of my life."

Johnny's face turned confused.

"What?"

"No man, like an hour after you left everything went fucking biblical! That dude who always comes in and has like, one beer for two hours then leave…"

"Trenchcoat guy?"

"Yeah Trenchcoat guy. He gets up, drops his coat, walks into the middle of the street and screams up to the sky 'If you want my blood you'll have to come here and take it.' We all thought he'd just snapped, finally gone over the deep end right? But then lightning just, just hits him, out of nowhere. And not like a strike, hits him and stayed. Check it out I took a video."

Josh quickly pulls his phone out and taps it a few times. Their TV suddenly lit up with images of a man standing defiantly with lightning arcing over his body, turning his shirt to ashes around him. His eyes glowing an electric purple. All at once he snatches the arc and pulls down hard, then as if it were an elastic band he catapulted into the sky.

Johnny turns a blank ghost pale stare at Josh.

"What, what does this all mean?"

"Oh no man, that's not the end. From there we all witnessed this titan battle in the clouds, as if Trenchcoat guy had become part of the sky until it looked like he'd gotten his hands around the neck of some other figure and snapped it, in what sounded like the loudest close explosive thunder crack I've ever heard."

"Oh my god, I heard that, that woke me up I just presumed it was a storm and, and just went back to sleep."

"No man, it was this battle in the sky. Anyway, no word of a lie, Trenchcoat begins to fall and slams into the sidewalk; only he just picks himself right back up, swings on his coat, drops five bucks for the beer and casually walks off, as if nothing had happened."

Johnny covered his eyes with his hands trying to wrap his mind around it, trying to work out what it all meant. Were the Gods real, how would he be able to reconstruct his reality now knowing that these kinds of beings existed. He suddenly felt very small and vulnerable. He wiped at his eyes and swallowed away the growing panic.

"Ok, so what does the pumpkin have to do with this?"

"Oh man, best part...

Johnny's fear levels rose and a slight sweat started.

"So on the way home I walked past the little 24-hour market, and they had pumpkins on sale. I got this baby for like 2 bucks."

Josh patted the massive pumpkin and smiled proudly, while Johnny's mouth dropped open.

"That's the best part? Your night involved literal Gods battling in the sky and that's the best part?"

"Yeah man, pumpkin soup, it's nutritious and delicious. It's awesome."

# Women

"Do you ever wonder what it'd be like to be a woman?"

Johnny stopped mid-sip of coffee, put his mug down and turned his full attention to his friend.

"What?"

"Like if you spontaneously became a woman right now, what do you think you'd do?"

"Go lock myself in my room until you stopped asking me if you could play with my boobs."

Josh looked down at Johnny's chest and for a moment his imagination distracted him, but he managed to shake it off.

"No but seriously."

"You're going to have to be more specific. Do you mean like, makeup and tampons or do you mean what work would be like? Or is this a discrimination conversation? What aspect of this discussion has you thinking about it?"

Josh opened his mouth but closed it again as he looked around his mind trying to find the root of the idea and come up short.

"I... I don't think I actually thought about it that hard, more of an idle thought about what it would be like, and before I had an answer myself I asked you."

Johnny finally took a sip of his coffee and turned his attention back to the TV.

"Freak out."

"What?"

"I think if I transformed into a woman, the first thing I would do is freak out. Because that sounds really terrifying. Not because I was suddenly a woman, but because the idea of spontaneously transforming into anything sounds really terrifying. After that, I don't know, probably call my mom."

"Oh good idea, get some perspective. Also, she did always want a daughter."

They both nodded knowingly and relaxed back into the comfort of a complicated discussing, skilfully dodged.

# Food Porn

Johnny rolled over still half asleep and jumped swearing as he saw his flatmate sitting next to his bed watching him and eating an apple.

"What the hell are you doing in my room?"

"I've been thinking about apples."

"That's not enough of an answer."

"Well, you know how Adam and Eve get kicked out of heaven for eating an apple?"

"Like how I'm about to kick you out of here now?"

"No hear me out; I was thinking what if it's metaphorical?"

Johnny sat up feeling more than a little confused about the conversation he was now being forced into having.

"It's a bible story, of course, it's metaphorical they all are, what's your point?"

"I was thinking that the apple is actually a representation of sex, I mean have you ever cut an apple in half, the core can really look like a vagina. It seems super obvious when you think…"

"Wait, wait, stop, no. Your ground-breaking theory that has you sitting in my room in the middle of the night, is that the story of the Apple and Adam and Eve is about sex, because a cut open apple, looks like a vagina?"

"Well yeah, the snake gets Eve to try it first, and then she talks Adam into it. So she starts playing with herself, Adam finds her and is tempted to join in."

Johnny's eyes grew wide with rage and after a long sigh he pulled his blankets up over his head, lay back down turning away from Josh.

"I hate you get out of my room and move out of this flat by the morning."

Josh feeling his point still valid walked around the bed to show the remaining half of his apple.

"No but look, and I mean if you really think about it makes sense."

"No it doesn't, kindly die."

"Don't be like that, anyway get some sleep and we'll discuss it more in the morning."

# Unexpected Events

Josh walked sleepily into the lounge and looked at his old roommate Mathew, who looked back at him and smiled.

"Hey man, how are you? You look a little out of it."

Josh yawned and rubbed his eyes.

"I'm alright, really weird dream though."

"Oh yeah?"

"Yeah, I dreamt that a demon leapt onto my bed out of the shadows, held me down and ran his nail over forehead while screaming that, if I wouldn't choose to see the truth he'd pry open my third eye and force me."

"That is pretty weird. What do you think it means?"

"I don't know but I figure it has to mean something."

"Why?"

Josh turned to his friend and a sad smile crept over his face.

"Well... because you died 2 years ago man."

"I did? Holy shit I did! What, what happened?"

"Do you remember Nadine?"

Mathew thought for a moment and found his memories seemed to exist behind a fog.

"Sort of, nice girl, from work? Shitty home life?"

"That's the one. You decided to help her out, went with her to her place to confront her boyfriend and tell him she was leaving. Needless to say a fight broke out between the two of you and..."

"And he killed me?!"

Josh sat quietly for a moment staring into nothing.

"No, she did."

"That doesn't make sense."

"You were winning the fight and the more you hit him, the more her fear of what he would do to her grew. You were the safest option to stop so she grabbed his gun and ... stopped you."

Mathew slumped back in his chair watching his memories clear as he listened and felt like he should shiver or shudder but couldn't.

"And now what, they're still together?"

"Oh no, she is very much in jail. He was taken to hospital but hasn't been seen since."

"I can remember just wanting to help, feeling like I was doing the right thing, a good thing, but, but it all turned out so bad. How is that possible? I wanted to help her and I just made it worse."

Josh let out a sigh and thought it over.

"Different, definitely, but as strange as it might sound, I actually think she's happier now."

Mathew turned an even more confused look on him.

"Well, everything she'd ever done was based on fear, abusive parents turned into abusive boyfriend, she lived her whole life afraid, but in prison, they can't get to her. She writes to me sometimes, it started out just letter after letter of apology and I replied and now I get one once a month. She genuinely seems calmer, happier, less afraid. It might not have been the hero moment anyone was expected, it's certainly not how it goes in movies, but I honestly think you helped that girl."

The confused look on Mathew's face stayed for a moment longer then everything about him seemed to ease and a smile the changed his whole face washed over him and he was gone, leaving Josh sitting on his couch blinking away the light and wondering if it had really happened, or if this was all still just a dream.

# Hawaii

"This is not what I had in mind when we were planning a tropical holiday."

Johnny was standing by the window staring out at the sheets of water falling from the sky and the bursts of lightning that seemed to erupt into spider webs across the clouds.

"What do you mean; this storm is so tropical it's practically a cliché."

"It's just not what I had in mind. I was thinking, you know. Girls in bikinis on the beach, swimming in the sea, cocktails and exotic fruits."

He turned to face Josh who grinned and reached into the basket next to him and produced a mango.

"That's not exactly what I meant either."

"Oh come on, sit down tea is almost ready."

Josh tossed the mango and stocked the coals under the kettle. The storm which had been raging for almost a week had taken out the power in the first few hours and, as far as they could tell, no one was really planning to do anything about it. Johnny slumped down next to his friend and let out a harrumph.

"It's not that bad, I mean, isn't this why we got a private cabin, to get the authentic Hawaii experience. This is it, man, embrace the adventure."

"I don't want the authentic Hawaii experience; I want the Girls Gone Wild Hawaii experience. I want to get so drunk that I don't know how I ended up wherever I wake up with people I don't know the name of. I want to scream 'spring break' at some dude with a video camera and regret it when I find it online the next day."

Exasperated he got back to his feet and started pacing around the room, unsure of what to do with himself, while Josh poured them both cups of tea.

"Man, the storm has to pass at some point, just give it a bit of time. We can still have that other wilder experience afterwards. Live in the now man, embrace island life."

Johnny drank some tea and let himself really hear his friend's words.

"Yeah, yeah you're right man. Ok, ok I'll chill."

As the days turned into weeks and the storm showed no sign of stopping, Johnny and Josh found that the more they embraced the world as it was, the calmer they felt, and when the mudslide came crashing through their wall, they were ok with it, they were at peace. Totally unaware that the tea they'd been drinking was an incredibly strong hallucinogenic herb, and that they were just on their couch at home watching documentaries.

# Tie Dyed Shirt

Johnny looked at his friend.

"I trusted you."

"I know, and for that I am sorry."

The two men stared at each other, one feeling malicious sorrow the other, helpless pity.

"I... I still don't understand."

"In the same way that the scorpion who asks the frog for a ride across the river will sting him, knowing they will both die. This is simply, in my nature."

Silence fell until finally Johnny let out a breath and announced.

"Bullshit! Metaphors are nice and all - but come on, you're a person like I'm a person. I'm sure you want there to be some higher meaning but there really isn't. Just tell me, why'd you set my shirts on fire?"

Josh sighed.

"Man? Really? They were so embarrassing. And not just for you but for me and for everyone else. Everyone who saw you was embarrassed."

"That's not true! They're awesome. They show off how open-minded and chilled I am."

"No, they showed off how much of a fashion victim you are, and how much you hope hippie chicks think you're cool."

They stared at each other for a few moments.

"But did you really have to set them on fire?"

"I think you know the answer to that."

"Ok, but did you have to set them on fire … in our kitchen?"

Another silent moment passed between them.

"I will admit.  I regret that the house burnt down, but I still think that ultimately, I made the right decision."

# Fremdscham

"I'd like to thank you all for coming here today; I would like to officially announce my candidacy for president of this great Island of ours. For too long have the good people of this country sat back and watched while the elite, and the entitled have assumed control and steered things in a way that suits them and no one else. Well, I say it's time to change all that. This country will no longer be ruled in favour of the minority elite but for the benefit of the people. For the benefit of you! I solemnly swear that if I am elected I'm going to make sure that everyone has access to good teachers, and doctors and food! Not just those who believe they are better and more deserving because they have money. If they're so rich, they can pay for it themselves and for once let the people in need actually get what they need to achieve, and not just... survive! I swear that if elected things are going to change and the people who will reap the benefits are the people putting in the work, the people making the sacrifices, the people of this great country. You, the people, are my highest priority!"

Josh reached across and switched off the television then turned to his flatmate.

"He does say some pretty good things that guy."

"Smart, articulate, shame his fly was down though."

"I know right, and who goes commando these days, so 90's."

"So 90's."

# Laughter

At five years old Johnny was the oldest person he knew. Unlike most people, whose brains stop recording when they went to bed, his continued like normal. Every time he slept he lived whole lifetimes in the dream world. His parents believe their special boy was just a bit airy and would settle, and at that point, he realised that he was the only one who lived like that; he'd also decided not to burden them with the knowledge. To him, the real world seemed a temporary place, where time passed very quickly and moments were exactly that. It was uncomfortable, crowded and chaotic. The dream world he lived in made much more sense, it was ordered and since he was particularly smart, it was also vast.

At age five he felt like he'd lived a thousand years, and pretending to be a child for 16 hours out of every few years was difficult. But he managed, mostly. He came across as a distant sleepy child who didn't interact with other children much and if caught off guard, spoke like a man his mental age which frightened adults and confused children. All things considered, his parents couldn't be blamed for what they did, they weren't to know that sending him for his first sleepover would have the effect it had.

Johnny although mentally old still suffered from a very limited set of life experiences. As much as the dream world affected who he was in the real world, the real world could affect the entire dream world. So during his first sleepover when Josh's elder brother put an aged 18 horror movie on, the first 30 minutes were all Johnny's mind needed to change him forever. That night the dream world was no longer safe and when he stopped to listen, he could hear the faint sound of laughter coming from, somewhere. As time dragged on and the oppressive feeling grew so did the laughter and his fear of it. Until finally he came face to face with a man who stared down at him and whispered.

"Don't play with me child. I will reach inside your mind and introduce you to *my* nightmares. And then, and then you will truly understand the meaning of fear."

And then he laughed that terrifying, haunting laughter that came from everywhere.

When Josh's parents woke up they were surprised to find their son's little friend sitting at the kitchen table drinking coffee and looking, old. Johnny had lost all inclination to play young. In his time asleep he'd learnt just how little he really knew about the world and encountered horrors that the real world couldn't possibly recreate. His dream world had become a nightmare filled hellscape that he knew he was destined to spend millennia in, fighting and suffering, save for his blessed moments of relief in the real.

"Good morning, I hope I didn't wake you, I was trying to be as quiet as possible. You don't mind that I helped myself, do you?"

He lifted up the coffee cup.

"Wonderful stuff this, I'm new to it but can already feel we're becoming friends."

A sad but genuine smile spread across his face as a few tears ran down his cheeks.

"I'm just so happy to be here, with you wonderful people. Being awake, being alive, it's so unbelievably beautiful here. Everything is just so …"

He let out a long sigh and then finished his cup with a few quick swallows then refilled it from the pot while Josh's parents stared on in surprise.

"You know, you two really are lucky to have each other, and the children. But you better keep an eye on them because let me tell you. One day you'll blink and they'll be moving out, starting their own families. Life is just so fleeting that way. But I suppose that's what makes it all so precious."

A soft laugh slipped out as he finished another cup.

"Well, I should probably get going. Can't spend all my time sitting here drinking coffee and waxing lyrical. The world is out there, waiting to be experienced. Gods!.. I just can't get over how beautiful everything is, don't you think?"

He looked at the two stunned faces of people who had, until that point, always considered Johnny to be a little slow. But he laughed again, jumped off his chair and left, set to walk himself home, hoping to take in as much of the real world as he could, before having to return to the hell of his own making.

# Burrito's by the River

Josh sat on the river bank and sighed and waved at Johnny who sat on the other side and grinned like an idiot.

"Why are we doing this again?"

Yelled Josh frustrated.

"For Science!"

Came the reply and Josh hung his head and swore. Then he watched as Johnny began to warm up his muscles in way that made it perfectly clear to everyone watching that he had no idea what he was doing, and was instead emulating people he'd seen prepare for a sporting event. He then fished a burrito out of his backpack and narrowed his eyes at Josh.

"Are you ready?"

Josh shook his head and let out a long sigh.

"Sure, fuck it, why not."

"You don't look ready!"

Shaking his head again Josh raised his hands and assumed a position that he decided would make Johnny satisfied that he was prepared to catch the burrito. He then let his mind wander away hoping to distract himself enough to not actually see what was about to happen. Johnny took a few steps back then with a running start, winding his arm back as he did and launched the burrito into the air with all his might just before he reached the edge of the river. Moving with such force that he couldn't even stop himself he dove head first into the water. The burrito flew in a beautiful arc in the sky spinning like an American football as it travelled to about halfway across the river and then it too, just as Josh had predicted, landed into the water never to be seen again. Johnny meanwhile, kicked and struggled to get his head out of the water and dragged himself back onto shore panting and spluttering and turned to look at his friend and then erupted into a cry of victory.

"I told you, I told you I could do it!"

Josh had waited until the perfect moment to retrieve his spare burrito from his own backpack, faked a smile and said sarcastically.

"How could I ever have doubted you?"

"Oh my God dude, this is the coolest thing that's ever happened, my single greatest achievement!"

"You have an actual, literal human child!"

"Doesn't even come close!"

Josh shook his head and started walking to the bridge to get to his friend who was practically in tears he was so happy.

"Here."

"Now for the taste test."

"Remind me again why we're doing this."

"Because burritos are amazing and they only way they could get more amazing is if they're truly earned them. And I think this one, is truly earned."

He quickly unwrapped it and took a massive bite, then let out a moan and shivered in a way that made Josh genuinely worry that Johnny was about to cum in his pants, and suddenly felt a very strange prickle of envy.

"Oh my God dude this might be the best thing anyone has ever put in their mouths. Want a bit?"

Josh's face turned a little revolted.

"No, thanks, you earned this one, you can have it."

Johnny took another big bit and let out another equally excited moan.

"I think I want all my food this way."

At which point Josh grimaced and sighed,

"Yeah about that, don't you think that if you did this with everything it would just become normal? Trying to capture and repeat a perfect moment can ultimately cheapen the honesty of the original event."

Johnny looked at him a little confused.

"If everything tasted that good then by comparison this meal would just be normal and not ... orgasmic."

"Yeah, yeah I guess that makes sense."

"Anyway, don't focus on trying to make the perfect moment happen again, enjoy it while it's happening."

Johnny smiled broadly, nodded his head in agreement and took another massive bite, and to show just how much he was enjoying the moment, moaned even louder.

# Forgotten Birthdays

"No, no, just, no. I don't care what anyone says, *The Great Gatsby* just isn't good."

Johnny sat resolute in his statement and waited for the reaction, which came quickly.

"How can you say that?"

"Easily, it's because old Scottie isn't a good writer."

Josh stood up and paced away for a few steps then turned.

"*The Great Gatsby* is a classic, you understand, *claaaaassic.* That means it is the very measure of what great writing is. It's a story that's stood the test of time, and the fact that we're still able to have this argument, how every many hundred years later, proves you wrong."

"Don't give me that, just because something is old doesn't give it merit. Just because some headmaster got bribed into making it required reading in high school doesn't actually mean its good literature. *Hemingway* on the other hand..."

"Don't you dare!"

Interrupted Josh,

"Don't you dare bring that bloated boring windbag into this. *F. Scott Fitzgerald* wrote poetry with vision and beauty while *Hemingway* wrote boring flat prose with no heart, no soul and no dimension. It's not comparable."

"But it's also a *claaaaassic*. So how can you defend one and hate the other?"

"Have you read *For Whom the Bell Tolls*? Of course you haven't, because no one has, no one can stay awake long enough to get past the first page!"

Johnny rolled his eyes in response which only annoyed Josh more and he flung his copy of *Gatsby* at him in a rage.

"Go on then, turn to any page, any section and read it and it'll prove you wrong. I don't need to defend it, it'll defend itself!"

Johnny took a deep breath to maintain his poker face, knowing exactly which part of the book to read that would prove his point best and burn down his friend's argument.

"...and I quote;

The Great Gatsby by F Scott Fitzgerald, Chapter 7:

*After a moment Tom got up and began wrapping the unopened bottle of whiskey in the towel.*

*"Want any of this stuff? Jordan? . . . Nick?"*

*I didn't answer.*

*"Nick?" He asked again.*

*"What?"*

*"Want any?"*

*"No . . . I just remembered that to-day's my birthday."* "

Josh stared at his friend in a rage so intense Johnny though he might actually attack him.

"I hate you."

"I didn't write it."

"That's not fair that's only one section out of the whole book and…"

"And you said the book could defend itself."

Josh started pacing up and down the room breathing heavily and Johnny suddenly wondered if he hadn't gone too far this time. They had had the argument before, not quite so intensely and Josh had never reacted so badly, and it made him wonder what was up. He also knew his friend well enough to know that the best thing to do would be to sit quietly and wait. Which he did for about 2 seconds before deciding that teasing him and seeing how much further he could push the situation actually seemed like much more fun.

"What, did you just remember that today's your birthday too?"

Josh let out a weirdly high pitched scream and dove onto his friend. The two wrestled for a solid minute before collapsing onto their backs on the floor next to each other, breathing heavily.

"We really need to get out more."

"I can't believe you actually attacked me."

"I mean, God damn, are we really this unfit?"

"Fuck you douche bag you attacked me."

Josh turned his head to look at Johnny.

"Yes well, you were being a dick."

"That's not the point."

Josh shrugged panting and reached out an arm across to pat his friend's chest.

"You deserved it, now stop saying horrible things about my favourite book or I'll … hell, I don't know, sneak up on you in the middle of night and cry on you."

Johnny's face contorted in horror and disgust.

"Jesus, that sounds.'

He shuddered as his skin erupted in goose bumps.

"*Really* awful."

They both let out tired laughs as they lay there panting for a few more minutes until Josh managed to say.

"How did we get into the argument again?"

"You came home and after finding a pile of free books on the street and asked me to name the greatest book ever written and I said The Lord of the Rings."

"Oh right, now I remember."

Another few moments passed as they lay on the floor until Johnny sat up, sighed and said.

"Hungry? I think we've still got some soup."

# Attachment

"Oh man, and then there was that girl, do you remember? What was her name?"

"Janet."

"Yeah, Janet that's right. I swear you could light cigarettes off her, she was HOT! Last night was epic!"

Johnny sat for a moment smiling at his friend, waiting patiently for the inevitable realisation and after a few minutes, it arrived. Josh's face changed in its usual subtle way, his eyes unfocused and refocused and looked at his friend questioningly.

"But it wasn't last night, was it?"

"No, that particular party was about sixty years ago."

"Sixty years, how, how is that possible we still look the same?"

Johnny let out a little chuckle.

"No my friend, we don't."

Josh looked down and for a moment saw himself, not as he was but how he used to be. But then his vision shifted and suddenly an old man sat there.

"Oh my God, but, how? What happened?"

"We got old is what happened. We continued to live together for far too long but eventually got our lives together. You got married had some kids, I didn't get married but also had some kids and we drifted into life. Coming together from time to time. Then as we settled into the final stages of life we decided to move in here and end life the way it started, together."

As he spoke Josh watched his friend age from the young man at the party to the old man he was now.

"I really got married?"

"Yeah, to Janet actually, I think that's why you always remember that party so clearly. It was one of the last we attended while living together."

"But where, where is she? What happened to her and my kids?"

Johnny pointed across the room at an old woman quietly reading a book and smiled, Josh recognised her instantly and his face lit up.

"And my kids?"

"They'll probably visit on Thursday, that's normally when they come round."

"And your kids?"

"Also Thursday, its visitor's day, besides, your son married my daughter."

Josh's mind flashed with memories of getting drunk at a wedding.

"Why, why don't I remember these things?"

"We're 89 years old. We forget things. But not always, and you always come back with a little encouragement."

Josh smiled at his friend and remembered a little more, remembered grandchildren sitting on a couch playing video games talking about moving into a house together and growing old together. He remembered how happy he was when they all moved into the care home and how now that they were old, it was acceptable to sit on the couch all day and sleep until the afternoon. And he remembered pumpkin soup.

# Layover

Henry finished his book and looked at his watch. Still 6 hours before his connecting flight. He sighed and started scrolling through his Kindle looking for something else to read. All at once his music stopped playing and the battery light on the Kindle started flashing. He looked around at all the people in the waiting area and realised there wasn't going to be a free power source for a while. Looking at his watch again he decided it was five o'clock somewhere. So he packed up his stuff and went in search of a bar. After many long boring corridors, he found a small airport lounge, mostly abandoned except for a woman sitting alone and the barman cleaning glasses.

"So, come here often?"

The woman turned a confused look towards him and was greeted by a charming but tired smile. She let out a little laugh and his shoulders relaxed.

"This might be the first time that line is ever going to work. Because no, this is my first time actually, what about you?"

He took up the seat next to her.

"Mine too, also it's the first time I've ever used that line, but so far 100% success rate."

The woman smiled and raised an eyebrow.

"You either have a lot of faith in your abilities to charm a woman, or don't fully understand the turn 'pick up line.'"

Henry blushed, suddenly realising what he'd said and fumbled over his next few words causing the woman to laugh again.

"Sorry no, that, that, that's not what I meant. God damn, I can't even blame alcohol."

"I know right, it's not like it's busy. I've managed to have exactly one glass of wine in an hour. I'm Amanda, by the way."

"Henry, nice to meet you, and let's see what we can do about that, Barman!"

The barman turned around to see both Henry and Amanda smiling broadly at him and sidled over. They got themselves some drinks and fell easily into conversation. They spoke about where they were from, where they were going, how long they were stuck in the airport, what books they'd read, the movies they'd watched on the flights. She made charming look effortless and he smiled every time she laughed at one of his silly jokes.

Henry gradually became aware that they were flirting with each other and that it was going really well. The tone of the conversation took on a more 'deep and meaningful' quality and their chairs shifter closer together so that their legs could rest against one another. Henry casually put his hand on hers and they locked fingers. An hour passed this way as they openly discussed their lives, hopes and dreams until finally, the conversation came to a natural break they both leaned forward and kissed.

The intercom system chimed and announced.

"Now boarding Flight SN1574 could all passengers please processed to Gate 42."

Amanda pulled away and rested her head on Henry's shoulder.

"Oh! What horrible timing!"

"Your flight?"

"Yip."

They sat in silence for a moment before she pulled herself upright and frowned.

"This is such bull shit, I've been single for ages, I've got two online dating accounts and now in the middle of nowhere in an airport you come along and we literally live on different sides of the world. It's not fair."

"I know imagine how my wife feels."

Amanda's hand slammed hard against the side of Henry's face with a loud crack and he sat motionless for a moment before opening his eyes.

"I was joking, just trying to ease the mood. Sorry."

Amanda quickly put her hands over her face.

"Oh god, I'm so sorry."

Henry smiled.

"No, it's my fault; I shouldn't have said it, bad joke, bad joke."

She gently rubbed the bright red handprint on his face, and a tear slipped from her eyes. Henry frowned and scooped her into his lap so he could wrap his arms around her.

"It's really not fair, I really like you, I haven't met anyone I've gotten along with so well and so comfortably … Well, ever actually."

The intercom sounded again.

"Second boarding call for Flight SN1574 could all passengers make their way to Gate 42 immediately."

"I really have to go."

They kissed again and Henry let her slip off his lap to her feet.

"Would it? …would it make sense to stay in touch, make a plan maybe?"

But even as he said it he found himself losing faith in the words, knowing that it didn't. They stared at each other for one long last second, then she set her jaw, picked up her bag and without a goodbye hurried off to her gate, leaving Henry once again alone in an airport waiting for his connecting flight.

# Godspeed

"My father had always told me that, at some point during the apocalypse, you have to put on the shoes you are going to wear for the rest of your life. As a child, I'd never really understood it, maybe because I thought I'd live forever or maybe because I couldn't grasp the concept of an apocalypse. As I got older and suffered through a few life experiences my understanding grew. I think what he'd been trying to tell me was that some choices can't be unmade. In the end, you have to make a choice and stick to it no matter what. So, when the day came where I had to flee my home and literally run for my life I paused for a moment while putting on my shoes and thought of my father. As the world around me literally exploded and buildings came crashing down I couldn't help but wonder if these would be the shoes I would wear for the rest of my life, and how long that might be. Of course, when a shell hit the building I was in and rock started to fall down around me I forgot all that, pulled on my shoes and ran with everybody else.

The war that had been raging for so long had finally left the newspapers and reached the border of my city. Even then it seemed unbelievable and although it wasn't an apocalypse in the biblical sense it certainly felt like one to us. As my neighbours and I ran through the streets with our homes and favourite shops, restaurants and bars exploding around us, I think we all would have agreed that it was the end of the world. If we had the time to think of course, which we didn't, we could only run. In hindsight, it was stranger than you'd think. In many ways, I felt more alive and more present than at any other time in my life. My thoughts were on the exact moment, every moment. My reactions were immediate to the world around me, and every time it changed I changed. It had to be that way, if you didn't you died. And not slowly, not like life said you would, where at the moment you stop changing to the world you begin to die. Not in a retirement home watching old television shows, talking about the days when the world made sense to you. You died right then, right at the moment, you didn't change with the world. It was the entire life condensed into a single moment, and every moment was another entire life.

We had been running towards a bunker that had been advertised on the news, but when we reached it, it was already gone, some stopped to scream and cry. We never saw them again. Other including myself simply kept running, aiming for the east side of the city, which happened to be across a river. No one thought of the bridge but anyone who'd lived in that city long enough had at some point swam that river. So that's what we did. We dove into the water and swam across, and once there we kept going. By the time the explosions sounded more like thunder than death, I was surprised to discover that it had only been 25 minutes. We had as a group stopped to catch our breath and I managed to spot my building just before it collapsed, and I thought again about my shoes and my father. Then I turned towards the journey in front of me, to the only option anyone could think of. Keep running until we find the next place and hope the war hadn't reached them and that there was enough civilisation there so that we could run further and faster. And so we did, we fled the city and kept going. Some stayed behind to try hiding, some spoke about fighting; some gave up along the way. But myself and a few others found good fortune in each other's company and kept going until we reached the next city. At that point we had decided that whatever we did we did it together, and so we pooled what money we could get and bought a car, warning everyone we met about the incoming invasion and then left to continue running away.

And eventually, we ended up here."

The man pointed at the small camp around him and smiled while the reporter busily wrote down notes. She looked up at him gravely.

"So what do you plan to do from here?"

"We've heard that they are letting in refugees at the northern border and giving safe haven, that the counter-attacks are finally working and there is hope the war will end soon. So we're sticking to our plan and heading north. We … we are not the people who started this war, we don't believe in it and we cannot end it, all we can do is run from it. It isn't the noble choice but it's the one that has kept us alive. And if there are no people left alive at the end, there will be no one to rebuild."

His smiled turned distant for a second and then they heard the call of his friends to start getting ready.

"Just one more question if that's ok."

"Of course."

The reporter smiled and closed her noted book.

"Are you still wearing the same shoes?"

# Bones

Edgar stared at the woman on the bus through the corner of his sunglasses and wondered what her skull looked like. It was something he'd only ever thought about himself, and only ever when feeling in a particularly strange mood. But now he found himself wondering about this woman on the bus. He then wondered if it was because some part of him thought they looked similar and then she shifted in her chair and he decided that no, they didn't. But still, he wondered what her skull looked like. The desire was so great in his mind that he was most of the way towards forcing himself to talk to her when she pressed the bell and got off, leaving him alone with his thoughts and 37 strangers, including the bus driver. It was only two stops later that he realised he was supposed to get off at the same stop as she did and as a result arrived slightly sweaty and a bit late to work. It wasn't late enough for anyone but him to care, but he did hate being late. So, although no one had noticed, he returned from lunch 15 minutes early to make up for being 10 minutes late. He was neurotic and he knew it, but he also accepted it. He made allowances where he'd let himself and tried not to beat himself up over it too much when his neurosis would allow. He also would give into them when he knew that fighting wouldn't work. So, he spent every morning for the next few weeks looking and hoping to spot the woman on the bus, and every evening standing naked in front of the mirror trying to imagine what his skull looked like. Then he'd take a shower and go to bed. He got no joy from any of it, but he knew that if he tried to stop himself, he'd just be locking himself into an internal argument that would prevent work and sleep and possibly get him back to a point of needing an intervention. So, on the 18th morning when the woman sat down next to him on the bus, he had to fight not to openly stare or say something creepy like.

"I think you have a nice skull."

Or,

"Hey, I've been hoping to see you here for over two weeks."

But did want to say something. She'd been leaning in on his thoughts for so long he felt he owed it to himself to try talking to her, even though he wasn't sure why. After a few minutes and just after the bus stopped to pick up its second load of too many people, he found himself scoffing and saying.

"Morning traffic, am I right?"

Which got no reply. For a second he wondered if he'd actually said it, then wondered if he'd only whispered it, and then saw the earphone wire coming out of her hair and breathed a sigh and stared out the window until he heard a woman's voice say.

"Jesus! Morning traffic, right?"

He turned quickly to see the woman holding her earphones and staring at the new horde of people cramming into the bus.

"I know right, it's like why don't they just send more buses on Monday to Friday."

The woman squeaked as she quickly turned to look at him and blushed crimson.

"Oh sorry, I thought I'd thought that."

Edgar blushed in response but quickly said.

"It's fine."

He turned again to stare out the window, mentally convincing himself that he would get off one stop later than usual so that he wouldn't have to suffer the stress of following her. He then started to pray that she'd get off at the stop he was thinking so that it didn't look like he was staying longer on the bus. Even though a part of him knew that she didn't know which stop he was meant to get off at. When she got up she left a few stops early, Edgar felt like he could breathe again for the first since their conversation. He then spent the rest of the morning wondering if she'd gotten off early because she was embarrassed, and then started plotting alternative routes to work so that he wouldn't bump into her again. Then he realised that if she had gotten off because she was embarrassed maybe she was looking for alternative routes too and him changing his path might actually increase the chance of seeing her and after many hours of that internal dialogue, he decided it was time to call his therapist. His paranoia had spread to beyond the boundaries of his understanding and he had become completely overwhelmed. He got signed off of work for three weeks, again and was checked into a care facility. This instantly made him feel a little better and a lot safer. That was right up until day three when a new patient arrived and he found himself staring at the woman from the bus, and once again started to wonder what her skull looked like. That afternoon he wept on the floor of his therapists' office while babbling incoherently about skulls and girls, to the point that the doctor starts to note down every word just to make sure Edgar wasn't confessing to a crime of some kind. It took a few hours but eventually, and with the help of some medication, they got him calm. Then after a few more days of very controlled supervision, Edgar agreed that he should in fact just talk to the woman. She, of course, was equally paranoid and neurotic and was equally confused and scared about seeing the man from the bus at her hospital. Although she had started to think that he wasn't real and in fact a hallucination that was following her around. But with guidance, time and the promise of trusted supervision, they met. The conversation was very slow to start, then became very quick and awkward and then descended into a strange comparison of disorders, medication and bus time tables. And, after an odd three weeks, they left together as boyfriend and girlfriend. A year later they became husband and wife and four years later were expecting their second neurotic child, who was so scared of coming out and facing the world that he had to be removed by force with Edgar watching his wife flatline in the birthing room. He found himself feeling like he was standing next to his body, watching everything from the outside and couldn't help but wonder if the doctors would let him see her skull.

# Normal

You have to smile, that's what they always told me. Smile and tell everyone that you're fine. Speak about positive achievement but don't brag, and never complain.

'Be nice.'

That's was my family motto, mantra. You have to be nice. Other people can complain and you will listen and be concerned, but don't get involved.

At 18 I will choose my career path, at 21 I will propose to the 'love of my life' and be expecting our first child by 23. We'll buy an apartment at 25. When I'm 35 my wife and our three children will move out of the city in our new house and I'll start commuting to work. On Friday nights I'll meet my 'friends' for a few beers and we'll discuss the week's sports results and debate politics. Every fourth Sunday we'll host a barbecue for those friends.

Two of the children will go to university and one will travel to Europe to 'find themselves'. My wife will battle breast cancer and win. I will act concerned about the mastectomy even though we haven't had sex in 20 years. I'll retire at 65 and take up gardening and finally make plans to visit the cities I've always spoken about on those Friday nights.

It's the perfect life.

The normal life.

It's the life everyone wants.

So

why

can't

I

stop


screaming?

# Questions

What if I'm actually too old?

Did I stop and think about the fact that one day I would no longer physically be able to carry on?

Did I ever consider that it would come this soon, or did I think it would just sort itself out one day?

What part of life did I get wrong? What simple misunderstanding and series of incorrect decisions got me here?

Did they really make sense at the time?

How fucking delusional am I?

Why can't I answer any of these questions!

What if ...

What if...

What if...

I've already failed, and I just don't know it yet?

# Circles

It was 7 am when his alarm started screaming, telling him he'd lain awake all night. The empty space beside him had proven too great a distraction. Although he and sleep had never truly been friends, they had always managed a workable love/hate relationship. As a child, his mind would spin in ever decreasing circles and it would keep him awake. Now it was the emptiness that held his attention. Too fixated on his own sorrow and self-loathing to even consider reaching out for something as soothing as sleep. Hot caffeine and cold showers were enough to get him up, and when they stopped working whiskey did the trick until it was time to lie back down and stare once again and the empty space beside of him. Part of him thought that perhaps if he drank enough he would simply black out or with some luck, die.

If only he were able to pull his mind away from loneliness for long enough, he could remember the metal box under his bed, but even that was too much, and the cycle continued. Finally, after three days and halfway through his fifth cup of coffee, a white light seemed to erupt in his vision. What seemed a moment later he was trying to pick himself up, wondering if it was coffee, blood or both that had glued his eye closed. Day had turned to night and almost back into day as he'd lain cold and alone on his kitchen floor. In the blur, his mind twisted and turned in small circles until it found a distant memory. And as he crawled to the shower to wash off whatever was covering his face, he let the memory grow. A way to break the cycle, to end the self-pity and wallow no longer. From the shower, he went to his bed, opened the metal box under neither it, took out the gun, put it against his temple and pulled the trigger. As his brains hit the wall beside him and his body the floor in front of him, his spirit sat motionless on the bed and for a moment stared at nothing. Then it lay down and fell back into thinking about the empty space beside him, waiting for 7 am, waiting to start the cycle all over again.

# Heritage

It was 4 years to the day that the letter arrived, four years to the day since the incident where my father, a quiet man with a strange sense of humour apparently lost control.

It had often been said that he used to tell himself jokes, because only he ever thought they were funny, and he often never spoke much above a whisper.

Until that day.

On that day the echoes of his actions could be felt across the world. I was younger then, but even now I don't fully understand or comprehend how a kind and quiet man could be associated with phrases like,

'A river of blood'

And

'Screams that I can still hear in my nightmare'.

And then the letter arrived and pieces of a puzzle I didn't want to build started falling into place. Receiving an apology from a dead man, but not the apology I expected. Not sorry for what he'd done in his last few hours but instead for who he'd been every day before that, for being a beacon of the mediocre, a harbinger of normal.

The phrase that stung most, like a slap to the ear read,

"I'm sorry that I was the perfect example of how you will fail, and I made it look so charming."

I stared at the letter my father had apparently written the night before

he 'lost control'

...and murdered 47 people,

and I realised that he was trying to force me to not be like him. That the worse thanks I could give him would be to emulate him, and I looked around from the desk he used to sit in, and I wept

...

As I reached for his gun.

# The Witching Hour

As a child her favourite thing was rain. If you asked her why, she'd say,

"It feels like the world is taking a shower, and when it's over everything is a little better, a little brighter."

So, when dark cloaks and masks burst into her house one night and dragged her off, a part of her prayed for rain. Hoping, wishing that it would come and wash away whatever horrors had grabbed her and save her from what would happen next. And although the rain came, it didn't wash them away. And for the next few years she was subjected to unspeakable acts, for the greater good. Faceless people proclaiming that the ends would justify the means, just as soon as they found the right means. As soon as they could prove themselves right, everything they were doing and would do and had done would become magically justified! And somehow that would make everything alright, like the rain. But it never happened, and a tortured little girl became a tortured young woman, and many of the faceless faces started to fear. One by one their fear of her transformed into fear of having to remove their masks and face up to what they had done, so in the middle of the night they would disappear and, in the morning, there were less faceless faces, until there was only one left. One solitary mask screaming accusations from the darkness. So blind to reality that it believed everything was somehow her fault, her doing. She had driven them away, made them disappear, and midnight was the key, midnight was her hour and it proved everything they'd believed for so long and finally justified everything they'd done, and justified what would happen next. Leaving her strapped to a bed as all of the evidence, all of the proof and all of her, was set on fire. As the smoke and the heat and the flame danced around the rooms, along the floors and up the walls to lick the ceiling, she once again thought of rain. Her friend, her lover, the only kindness in her life. She closed her eyes and prayed for it, wished, hoped, begged, screamed for a storm to come and wash away the flames, and the pain and the madness, to make everything ok and carry her back to being a child before any of the uncountable, unspeakable things had happened. But the rain did not come, even though the distant clocks struck for midnight, and when the flames finally flickered out it took her with them. Leaving only the faceless face alone to not stare at what had happened, at what had been happening for years. Frantic to tell themselves that no rain was no indication of mistake. Fire was the cure-all, everyone knew that. It was the fire that had prevented the rain. They were fine. They were justified. They had done the right thing. Saved the world from darkness, from evil, so that now, little girls everywhere wouldn't have to fear being taken in the middle of the night and used. Saved from having unspeakable things done to them. They had been right, they had to be right. Then, like everyone else, the final faceless face disappeared into the darkness, leaving behind only ashes and fear.

# Cyber Bullying

If it isn't funny, is it still a joke?

If you cannot feel it, is it still a poke?

I won't like that,

But I like that.

And if you disagree with me,

You're a, that other side pussy.

Leftist, rightist, Armchair philanthropist,

An, I'll give you a thumbs up while putting you down, ist.

I'm outraged at your outrage and my mediocre discomfort.

My first world problems matter too! Hashtag.#

So come at me bro, I can type like lightning,

Yeah! I'll bring up old tweets, what you gonna do?

I'll school you six ways from Sunday son!

You won't know which way is up when I'm done!

So welcome to the internet!

Where we're All Right, and you are wrong!

# Pirates

Jack hung over the side of his new boat throwing up everything he'd ever eaten in his whole life, or at least that's how it felt to him. In between each retch and heave, he took a moment to wonder what made him buy a boat, curse the man who sold it to him, and curse his brother even more for talking him into the idea of being 'an adventurer'. Thomas, on the other hand, was loving every moment. He'd spent the morning with the crew trying to learn all the terms and knots and anything he could. He'd helped put up the sail, even steered the ship out of the dock. He was now sitting on the deck next to his brother excitedly explaining his big plan.

"…You'll see Jack, once you get your sea legs, you'll see, this is the best decision you've ever made. We would have died at those desks working for Mr Tealeaf. Now we're our own men. Fortune awaits us."

"Die."

"Oh don't be like that."

"Kill me."

"Oh get off, you'll be fine! Here, I'll get Tiny to carry on down to your room and fetch you a cup of water and when you wake up everything will be fine."

Thomas jumped to his feet and waved a hand at the largest man on deck, whose name was actually Johnathan Small, but Thomas had instantly decided that he should, in fact, be renamed Tiny, and so that's what he called him.

"Tiny, please take my brother to his bed and fetch him some freshwater, and probably a bucket."

"Yes captain."

Tiny effortlessly lifted Jack onto his shoulder and carried the ever-greening man below deck. Annoyingly, Jack discovered that lying down and drinking some water did make him feel better but was reluctant to give his brother the credit of being correct. It had been a frantic morning organising everything and making sure they were fully and correctly stocked before departure. Thomas was good with people and the crew, but lousy when it came to forms, paperwork and organisation, which is where Jack truly excelled. Between a morning of heavy organising and an afternoon of constant vomiting, he thanked Tiny from the bucket and decided to let the gentle sway rock him to sleep.

To Jack's further annoyance, Thomas was once again right about getting sea legs and found that in the morning he could walk around quite easily with far less nausea, on top of that his brothers continued enthusiasm had become infectious. By the end of the day, Jack was once again confident about their choices and excited for their adventure.

Four weeks later and with no land in sight, even Thomas had started to feel the strain of ship life, and no wind was making it hard to stay enthusiastic.

Jack looked up as the door to his room opened and Thomas stepped in.

"Well brother, I have good news and bad news."

Jack frowned,

"What's the bad news?"

"There's a massive storm approaching."

Jack flushed a shade of green.

"W-what's the good news?"

"Storm clouds mean wind and land, and land out here means that the map I found is right."

"Wait - found? You told me you'd bought it."

"Yes, well, that was a lie, buuuuut, looks like it was correct so, no harm done."

"No harm done! We sold everything to fund this adventure of yours! Risked everything on a map you found! Where did you find it?"

"Underneath a drunken privateer outside the dockside pub."

For a moment Jack considered throwing something heavy and sharp at his brother but the approaching storm was far more the critical matter. He frowned deeply and levelled his gaze.

"This conversation isn't over. Now get the men from downstairs and make them do whatever needs to be done during a storm."

"Tiny said you'll need to lock up your cabinets and books and papers in the chests so that they don't fly around during the storm."

Jack nodded and started doing exactly that while Thomas got the ship and crew organised. The storm hit with a bang as water and hailstones slammed into the deck, and winds so strong that for a moment Jack thought the ship might take off flying. He had managed to lock everything away and with Tiny's help had secured himself and his bucket to a bedpost, but that didn't stop him from lifting off and bring thrown around whenever the ship suddenly dropped off a wave. Thomas, on the other hand, was on deck at the wheel catcalling the storm and riding the ship like a surfboard along the waves. With every insult he hurled at the clouds and lightning, the crew crossed themselves and prayed a little harder. But the smile on his face only grew with every crashing wave and as lighting narrowly missed striking the mast his laugh was loud enough to be heard by the whole crew. Eventually though, after what felt to Jack like days, the storm broke, and the ship and sea settled down enough for him to untie the rope and stagger up on deck to confront his brother. Thomas stood triumphant, pointing out to sea with a now smug smile. Jack followed his brother's arm to see an island on the horizon growing larger.

"Oh balls; there will be no living with you now."

"I knew that map was real."

"Did you really steal it off a man asleep outside the dock pub?"

"Well, he wasn't using it."

"And that's why we had to make plans and leave at such short notice, in case he figured out who took his map? Because it's possibly a treasure map that you stole from a pirate?"

"Yes, well, pirates are criminals."

98

"So what does that make us?"

Thomas's smile broadened.

"Adventurers."

# Diversity

As the brothers stared out across the water to the island, they heard a faint sound drifting across the water. After a moment, and seemingly at the same time they realised what they could hear was someone screaming for help. Frantically they began scanning the water for the source of the sounds and after a minute Jack called out.

"Over there, look, it looks like a lifeboat."

Thomas ran to his brother's side to look where he was pointing.

"Tiny, hard to port, there's someone stranded out there."

Tiny spun the wheel and Thomas turned back to the water and screamed: "We're on our way, don't worry!"

It didn't take long before they were close enough to the small boat to see a woman sitting in the middle of it, dressed in a strange black dress, decorated with bones and small animal skulls. The crew instantly crossed themselves and started to chatter in a way that made Thomas and Jack nervous. Tiny was quickly appointed the spokesman.

"We must turn the ship away from her, Sirs."

Jack narrowed his eyes.

"And why must we do that?"

"She's... She's a woman."

"I'm glad you were able to notice that Master Small, but now tell me, why does that mean we can't help?"

Jacks voice was flat and bordering on angry.

"It's, its bad luck to bring a woman on board."

"So we leave her to die? That's going to put us in better standing with God?"

Tiny shuffled his feet nervously.

"But sirs, she's... she's a..."

He looked back at the other crewmen then leaned in close to the brothers to whisper.

"She's a witch."

Thomas put a reassuring arm around Tiny's massive shoulders.

"And your plan is to abandon her to the ocean after we've already pledged to help? You think that's going to bring us better luck?"

Jack let out a long breath.

"No, we will do no such thing, bring the ship around and drop anchor. We're picking her up and that's final. If you and the others don't want to deal with her directly that's fine, we'll get her and she can stay in my room."

"But, Sirs -"

"But nothing, if you and the other men are scared of her then you can all go down into the hold while we get this done."

After a moment Jack added.

"Master Small I'm surprised at you. Superstitious and willing to leave a woman to fend off the sea on her own."

Jack's voice had taken on the hard tone of anger in a way that even surprised his brother. Tiny lowered his head embarrassed and followed the crew off the deck, leaving Jack and Thomas alone to steer the ship. Thomas waited until everyone had left before turning to his brother.

"Do you think she's really a witch?"

"I don't know, let's ask her."

It was harder having to do everything on their own but between the two of them, they managed to get their ship close enough to the small boat so that they could get the woman on deck and then quickly into Jack's cabin.

"Thank you, both so much for helping me. I thought I was dead for sure, and even when I saw your ship I wasn't sure if you'd actually come and help me."

Jack smiled,

"No, we couldn't just leave you out there, but how is it you ended up all the way out here on that little boat?"

"I live on the island you can see in the distance and I take my little boat out to fish, then the storm hit and pulled me out to here."

The woman and Jack stared at each other for a few moments in silence until Thomas, rolling his eyes, butted in.

"So are you a witch?"

"Thomas!"

"What? You're the one who said we could ask her."

The woman looked at the two men and realised that she felt no threat or judgement coming from them and so she smiled and said.

"Yes, yes I am. Is that a problem?"

Jack turned back to look at her,

"Not from us, and we'll keep the crew away from you so not from them either."

"That's incredibly kind of you, but aren't you scared I'll curse you, or remove parts of your body while you sleep to cast dark magical spells?"

"Not particularly, no."

The woman tilted her head quizzically.

"Our mother was a witch."

"Was?"

"She died when we were children."

"I'm sorry to hear that. May I ask what happened?"

Jack's face grew serious and a little sad as he turned to Thomas who had always been better at talking about it than him.

"Father said he was protecting us from discrimination and damnation. He turned her in, believing the courts would help her, fix her. Which they did first by half drowning her, and then by tying her up and setting her on fire."

"Oh my Gods, that's horrible, how do you know they tried to drown her?"

Thomas sighed and turned away blinking memories out of his mind, and Jack choked out.

"We... we were forced to watch."

A silent tear rolled down the woman's face and a small piece of her heart broke for the two small boys who still lived inside the men that stood before her.

"So we vowed to each other that we would never judge someone based on what people said they were, but instead on who they showed us they were."

The room went back to silence as they all let the dust of memory settle.

"My name is Isabella by the way, and I am very grateful for that vow. Also one of your crewmen is listening at the door."

Thomas frowned and quickly pulled it open causing Tiny to tumble headfirst into the room

"How much of that did you hear?"

"Enough to want to make the same vow Sirs, and to apologise for my actions."

"Accepted and forgiven. Now, we need to get her little boat onto the deck and get ourselves to that island."

"Yes sir."

"And please make sure that cook adjusts for an extra person on board."

"I will do so personally."

Tiny climbed to his feet, bowed towards Isabella and left to get back to his duties. Jack turned to Isabella.

"How did you know he was there?"

"I can hear thoughts."

"Oh? Oh... Oh, I'm uummm..."

Isabella giggled and smiled.

"Apology accepted."

# Escape

Tiny suddenly burst back through the door which slammed behind him.

"What's the meaning of this?" yelled Jack.

Tiny looked up, scared.

"Mutiny sir! The men are too scared of the witch."

Tiny suddenly blushed realising what he'd said in front of Isabella. But sanity quickly returned as the sound of crashing iron and wood filled the room, telling everyone that the door had been blocked. Thomas quickly helped Tiny back up.

"So what are they doing?"

Tiny's eyes grew wide with fright but before he could speak, Isabella's voice cut in small and scared.

"Oh no."

Then there was a crash, a bang and the unmistakable woofing of erupting flames.

"They're burning down my ship!"

Exclaimed Jack and Thomas simultaneously.

Then they looked at each other, worried.

"Jack, what do we do?"

All eyes in the room quickly turned towards the man who was so seasick on his first day that he had to be put to bed. Jack stared back at them for a moment racking is mind for a solution.

"Windows, we can get out through the windows."

He turned to Isabella.

"How far, roughly, are we from land?"

A nervous look spread across her face.

"Too far to swim, besides I umm... I can't."

"Can't what?"

"I can't swim."

"But you take a boat out fishing everyday... Never mind, ok plan B."

Jack once again looked into his mind, now with even more frantic desperation, then a light came on and an idea appeared.

"Tiny, Thomas, grab the heaviest thing you can find, we're going through the floor. The food store should be right below us, we get down there then we storm the deck and take back our ship and put out these fire!"

Without question or second thought everyone in the room grabbed whatever they could and started beating at the floorboards until they began to break and a big enough hole was created. Tiny jumped down last after making sure everyone else had gotten down safely. From there they all ran back up on deck expecting to find some confrontation but instead, the deck was empty. The fire raged around them and in front of them was a tide of life rafts as the crew fled the burning ship.

"What do we do now?!"

Yelled Thomas, and once again attention turned to Jack who looked at their livelihood in flames around them.

"Grab something that we can use as oars and get onto Isabella's boat. There is no way men this superstitious got on a witches boat!"

Tiny arrived behind them with a few long planks he had pulled from Jack's bed and the four of them jumped down into the small boat still tied to the side of their ship. As soon as all were aboard they rowed furiously toward the island to get away from the blaze and as they got closer to land both Jack and Thomas took a moment to stare at their fortune in flame and wonder with a growing sense of fear and dread what they would do now.

# Why Are Tears Salty?

Jack and Thomas sat back down in the middle of the small boat, letting their minds continue to drift in decreasing circles towards despair, while Tiny silently rowed them towards the island. Isabella sat with her eyes closed for a few minutes listening to the sounds around her and feeling the growing sense of dread coming from the two men.

"When I was a little girl, my mother - who taught me to be who I am - told me a story. I had had an argument with a boy from the town we lived in then. He had taken away my only doll, said I used it for black magic and threw it on a fire. I was so angry that I threw rocks at him and cried. My mom came when she heard me screaming at him, swept me up and carried me down to the beach. There she held me and told me that all things that are alive came from the sea. That the first people were born in the water but eventually, as all children must, they left their home to explore the wonders that could be found on land. But the sea continued to love her children, and she remained in their hearts. My mother told me the proof of this came with our tears, which are salty like the water of the sea. And that when we cry our true mother, the sea, comes to us and reminds us that no matter how far away we are, she is always there with us when we are sad, or when we are happy."

The three men stared at Isabella who stared back at them with a gentle smile. Jack cleared his throat and sighed.

"That's... that's a very sweet idea Isabella but -"

But Isabella held up a hand.

"I am telling you this not because it will help you in any physical way, but I always remember this story when I lose something precious to me. It doesn't help bring the thing back but I am comforted knowing that no matter where I am, I am connected to the love of the sea, and I hope that it might too comfort you two now as you have lost something precious, and to know that although you have lost your thing, you still have the love of the sea."

Jack and Thomas looked and each other and a sad smile slipped across their faces. In a moment they remembered that they had escaped alive and had each other, and Tiny and Isabella.

"Thank you."

# Trees and Deafness

The sun had already set by the time they landed on the island and it gave them enough cover to sneak off into the forest away from the crew. Jack was worried about what the men might try and do to Isabella since she survived the ship fire. She led them all through the woods to her small cabin.

"Please come in and make yourselves comfortable. I know it's only small but it should do for now."

"Thank you,"

"That's very kind of you."

"It's the least I could do; you've saved my life twice today."

"I... I am sorry about the way my men reacted, I thought they were better than that."

Thomas dropped his gaze to hide the red flush on his cheeks, feeling ashamed at having been the one who hired most of them. Isabella smiled at the brothers again.

"Good men do bad things when scared. You saved my life and have been incredibly kind to me, you have no reason for shame, I assure you."

Thomas looked up again smiling and set about helping Tiny start a fire, hoping Jack would take the opportunity to try his hand at flirting a little.

"This is …. Uummm a lovely cabin you've got. What brought you to this island?"

"Shipwreck actually, my mother and I eventually fled the town we lived in. We stowed away on a ship headed for the new world, but a storm appeared out of nowhere and lightning struck the ship setting it ablaze. My mother put me on a life raft and dropped me in the sea and the storm carried me here. That's actually how I got my little boat. Tiny looked up wide-eyed from the fire.

"And your mother?"

"I… I don't know, the men were trying to fight the fire but I was swept away and out of sight so quickly I couldn't see if they succeeded. You are actually the first people I've seen in almost two years."

Jack frowned.

"You've been alone on this island for two years?"

"No, not alone. I'm kept company by the forest spirits and the creatures who live in it."

Jack smiled and wanted to say something sweet but before he could think of anything he saw Isabella's face turn grave.

"What is it?"

"Your crew, they're…. they're…"

Suddenly they could all hear the sound of loud voices coming from outside the cabin.

"They're here!"

She finally managed to say.

"Run!"

Yelled Jack and they once again took off into the darkness. Thomas was the fastest runner so took the lead, making sure not to go too far ahead. Tiny, although not the slowest kept up the rear in case the crew found them. As they ran, Thomas realised the woods around them were growing thicker and darker and seemly out of nowhere Isabella's hand grabbed him urging him to stop.

"We must stop please."

"What? Why?"

"This is the haunted forest, we can't go further."

Jack panting looked at the now frightened woman.

"Why?"

"It is said that from here forward as the woods get thicker, darkness lives and the trees are possessed by evil spirits."

"Said by whom? You just told us you're the only person who lives here."

Isabella's face took on a slightly annoyed look.

"By the friendly spirits of this island, obviously."

Jack looked at Thomas, worried.

"What choices do we have, evil spirits ahead and apparently bloodthirsty mutineers behind us?"

As they looked back they saw lights from the crew's torches continue to draw closer and Jack took Isabella's hands.

"You're just going to have to ask the good spirits to protect us."

# Circles

He then nodded at Tiny who scooped her up and they continued to run deeper into the forest. Within seconds a chill gripped them, and the darkness seemed to grow oppressive, but they kept running until they could no longer see the crew. Then, as they began to turn around, they found they could barely see anything except for the massive trees that now surrounded them. Jack locked eyes with Thomas and opened his mouth to speak but either no words came out, or the sound simply didn't travel. Thomas frowned and Jack took on a look of surprise as he tried again to speak and nothing. Still confused, Jack began clapping his hands and found it made no sound. Tiny quickly put Isabella down and tried to ask her what they were going to do now, but since no sound could be made or heard she simply stared at him blankly. She then turned her attention to the trees around them and her lips began moving quickly and her hands started making small but precise gestures. A faint memory began growing in the back of Jack's mind and without hesitation he grabbed both his brother and Tiny's hands and ushered them to do the same, forming a circle around Isabella. As soon as it was formed a wind began, picked up and started to swirl, picking up leaves and sticks and dirt from the ground and flicking around them creating a vortex. Isabella raised her hands and dropped to her knees. By the way her mouth moved Jack thought if they could hear her she'd be yelling as the wind only grew stronger. Suddenly Isabella slammed her hands on the ground and for an instant, her eyes seemed to shine an electric violet and the darkness broke and they could hear her panting. Unsure of if it would work Jack first cleared his throat to see if it made a sound then said

"What... What did you do?"

She looked at him with her usual smile.

"I asked the good spirits to protect us. But how did you know to make a circle?"

"As we said, our mother was also a witch."

The two brothers smiled at the woman while Tiny began to shuffle his feet nervously.

"What are we going to do now?"

Jack's expression turned grave and he looked at his brother.

"You've got the map?"

"Of course."

"Then we're going to go find us some buried treasure."

Jack took the map from his brother and handed it to Isabella.

"Does anything on this mean anything to you?"

She looked over the map for a few minutes while the others simply stared at her expectantly. It gave a rough outline of the island itself and a list of cryptic clues, clearly intended to only be understood by its author. But Isabella had lived on the island long enough to understand some of them.

"I think this part here about 'beware the darkness' refers to the woods we're currently standing in, and if that's right then this part here, 'thunder on a clear day', Is talking about the cliffs on the other side. Which means your treasure is in one of the caves there."

Thomas's face lit up with a smile of success.

"Fantastic! So lead the way. That treasure is as good as ours."

But Isabella didn't look as enthusiastic.

"Well, not really, the caves there are pretty much impossible to get to."

"What? Are you sure?"

"Yes, I've tried a few times and failed, and without a rope it is impossible."

Smiles quickly faded.

"But, but there has to be away. Does the map not explain how to actually get to the treasure?"

Jack, Thomas and Tiny all joined in staring at the piece of paper. Minutes passed as they searched for clues until Tiny pointed down at it.

"What about this little circle here? What could that be?"

Next to it was a small note saying. "God doesn't make circles."

Again attention went to Isabella.

"That could be ... that would explain a lot. The cliffs are north of here, but northeast of us is a small clearing where the spirits don't go. There is a large round flat rock there in the middle. Perhaps that's covering a safe entrance into the caves?"

Jack and Thomas smiled at each other.

"That sounds like buried treasure talk to me. Lead the way; let us go find where a circle marks the spot."

# Derailment

It didn't take them long to find the small clearing and the large round stone, and between Jack, Thomas and Tiny they managed to lift it with ease.

"By the Goddess."

Exclaimed Isabella, as the moved stone revealed a small dug hole with a ladder leading into a tunnel. The excitement started to bubble up in the four of them as the idea of actual hidden treasure grew in their minds and they all quickly made their way down the ladder.

"It looks like you might have found us a genuine treasure map after all Thomas."

"What? You mean you doubted me?"

"Only constantly."

The brothers smiled at each other as they made their way deeper into the tunnel. After a few silent minutes of contemplation, a thought crept out of Thomas.

"It might have been my map, but you got us here."

"What are you talking about now?"

"Without you, none of this would have happened. I mean, sure, I dealt with the men, but you did all of the hard work, the mental heavy lifting, without you, I'd be nowhere."

"Our ship is either ash in the wind or coal at the bottom of the ocean, we're being hunted by mutineers on a haunted island. We're not exactly in a good space here."

Thomas reached forward and punched his brother in the leg in protest.

"Yes, but you got our expedition started, you get the ship in the first place, you got us off the ship while it burned and you remembered about circles while Isabella was casting her spell. If it were up to me I'm not sure we ever would have left England, let alone made it this far."

Jack knew what his brother was trying to say and he was touched, but also didn't really know how to respond, so was relieved when he saw that the tunnel they were in joined onto a much larger cave filled with sunlight.

"Looks like we've found the caves we're after, come along."

The cave was high enough that they all could stand and without much looking around they realised the term 'buried treasure' wasn't exactly accurate. Piled up in the back of the not very deep cave was what looked like a dragon's horde. Chests overflowing with gold and jewels, artwork, swords and guns, books and maps. It was more treasure than they could ever have imagined

"My God Jack we've done it! We're RICH!"

Thomas shouted as he jumped up and down in excitement. Grabbing his brother's hands he danced with him through the cave, singing.

"We're rich. We're rich."

Taken by the pure enthusiasm, Tiny and Isabella quickly joined in on the dance. But ever the sobering voice of reason Jack was the first to break away from the spell and stepped away from the group.

"The question is, how do we get this, and us, off this island and home?"

The dancing quickly stopped as the seriousness of their situation started to sink in. Tiny and Thomas looked at each other and then to Isabella, who had been living on the island for years and never found a way off. Or perhaps never looked for one. Isabella was looking at Jack who had suddenly grown contemplative and wandered towards the mouth of the cave to look out over the water. In the distance, he could see a small part of their ship sticking out among the waves. The cave fell silent for a few minutes and all eyes moved to Jack, waiting for him to once again come up with a solution. Jack continued to stare out at the water clearing his mind of distraction and running through possible solutions, ways to make a plan, looking at potential outcomes. Then suddenly it hit him and he turned to face the others with a smile on his face and his hand raised in triumph. But before he could announce his plan his body suddenly stiffened and his eyes went blank. He dropped to his knees for a moment then fell on his face. Thomas instantly ran to his brother, rolled him over and shook him.

"No, no Jack, no, no, no, please don't let this be happening... JACK! JACK!"

As he shook his brother's body blood started running from the hole in his head onto Thomas's legs.

"Jack no, don't leave me, please don't leave me."

Behind them, the mutineers had found the uncovered entrance to the tunnels and followed them in, without a word one of the men had fired a shot, originally intended as a warning, but had stuck Jack between the eyes. Before Thomas could even begin to form thoughts, Tiny wrapped a massive arm around him and leapt out of the cave mouth towards the water, Thomas over his shoulder and Isabella, screaming, under his arm.

# Trip Into The Unknown

As the trio hit the water Isabella's body begins to twist and thrash in the blind panic of someone drowning. But luckily, she was no match for the bone-deep strength of Tiny who had been born on a coastal town and got his first ship job as a cabin boy and look-out at the age of 9. He had learnt how to swim in the sea and knew how to save people who were panicking. As he pulled them all up to the surface of the water Isabella scratched at his arm and chest, screamed and kicked and did everything she could to make the situation worse until Tiny's large hand came down flat and hard against her face knocking her senseless and in that blur managed to find her calm. Thomas, on the other hand, did nothing. Didn't panic or struggle or swim. He just floated blank and unthinking, but Tiny had him too and with both under his massive arms started swimming with all his strength towards the shore.

Tiny continued to hold onto them both as he strode up the beach and once safely out of the surf dropped exhausted to his knees, finally letting them both fall onto the sand. Isabella shook with cold and fear.

"You, you saved our lives."

Tiny looked at his friends and smiled weakly, too tired and too sad to form words. Being out of immediate danger gave him the time to think about what had happened. Isabella knew what he was thinking and they both turned to look at Thomas who still stared blankly at the sand in front of him quivering. Slowly she managed to get to her feet and walk towards him.

"Thomas?"

He turned quickly, his eyes red with tears and a touch of insanity.

"Oh my god, where's Jack?"

"Wh-what?"

"Where's Jack, did we just leave him up there?"

"Thomas, Jack was shot?"

"And we just left him up there!"

Thomas turned his attention toward Tiny.

"What were you thinking just grabbing us, how could you leave him!"

Tiny turned a confused look towards Isabella, who tried again even more gently.

"Thomas, breathe, you're in shock."

But Thomas sprang to his feet, furious and determined.

"Get up, we've got to go and rescue him."

But no one moved, causing the redness in Thomas's eye to brighten.

"That's an order Mr Small! Get your lazy! Useless! Arse up!"

Isabella quickly put a sympathetic hand on Tiny's shoulder.

"Thomas."

"Thomas? Thomas? Thomas... Is that all you can say? Get up we're going after him."

"But Jack's dead, Sir."

Tiny's voice was sad, but matter of fact, and it seemed to strike Thomas, dropping him back to one knee.

"No... No! He's not!"

Thomas pushed himself back up.

"Right, if you two cowards won't help I'll go myself."

And Thomas turned and started running at full speed into the woods towards where he believed the clearing and the entrance to the cave was. Instantly Isabella and Tiny took off after him yelling.

"Thomas, stop, come back!"

"NO!"

Tiny pushed as hard as he could but could feel his legs and body start to give up and couldn't keep his speed going, while Isabella simply wasn't as fast as the madman in front of them, and after a few quick twists and turns, he was gone into the woods. Tiny stopped once he caught up with Isabella and sat down panting, his vision a blur.

"S-sorry m'lady. I... I'm so tired."

She sat down near him and put her arm around him.

"It's alright Tiny, I know, and you're not any of those things he said."

"Oh I know ma'am he's just got the sads."

She smiled for a second trying to ward of her own sad thoughts.

"We must go after him though; we know where he's going."

Tiny took a deep breath and pushed himself back up.

"Yes ma'am."

It didn't take long to get to the secret tunnel, but longer than they would have liked and as they crept closer to the entrance into the cave, they could see Thomas lying over the body of his brother, not moving or making a sound, and could hear the whispers of the mutineers from deeper in.

Isabella and Tiny stared at each other searching for some idea of what to do next, when Tiny's fatigue returned with a vengeance. Suddenly he slumped forward and fell to the edge of consciousness, leaving Isabella with what she felt like her only option. She remembered again the teachings of her mother and how they had always guided her, and she thought of the night they had escaped the town she was from. She closed her eyes and started whispering to herself. She then reached for her back and undid the laces that held her dress up. Tiny, seeing that she was moving tried to focus and looked up in time to see her dress fall to the ground, revealing her naked body. He quickly realized that she was covered in an intricate pattern of tattoos and scars, and as he continued to stare they began to faintly glow violet. Then, as if she had never been there, she simply vanished. Confused and exhausted Tiny lay his head back down and fell unconscious.

Isabella moved cautiously through the Unknown towards where Thomas lay over his brother, unsure of what she would find there. She had been scared of venturing into the Unknown ever since she and her mother had been separated, in case she found her there and confirmed what she feared over all else.

"Isabella?"

She turned quickly towards the sound and saw the glowing outline of a familiar form.

"Jack?"

"Isabella where are we?"

Her face turned grave and she looked down.

"We're in the Unknown, the world between worlds."

"How did we get here?"

She began to focus on him and willed him to remember. For a few seconds his glowing form took on more detail and for just a moment she could even see his face clearly.

"Oh? Oh... I... I ... We were in a cave, we had found the treasure. We needed a plan to escape. I... I was thinking... I?"

His form faded back into a glowing outline.

"I remember. How is Thomas, how are you all? Oh my God, if you're here does that mean?"

"No! No, I'm here by magical mean, but we are in danger. Tiny got us out of the cave, but Thomas refused to believe and ran back to find you. Tiny used up all of his strength saving us, and now he cannot help and here I am, once again seeking your guidance, hoping that that plan you had could save us still."

Jack sat back down on the shadow of a rock and searched through his mind.

"Originally I was going to suggest offering to pay the mutineers to come back to our serves and help build a ship. Remind them that they were stuck here too. Not sure that would work now."

Isabella's hope began to drop and a slow helpless feeling started making its way into her heart, and she whispered.

"Then I don't know what we are going to do."

"Isabella, if you have the power to ward off dark spirits and travel to this… Unknown, can you not use magic to save my brother yourself and Tiny?"

"My magic is all about spirits, my mother taught me this so that I might one day help people who are trapped to move on. I… I'm afraid I can do very little to affect the real world."

Suddenly a wind danced through the Unknown around them and a voice familiar to Jack whispered in their ears.

"Don't be afraid."

They both began looking around searching for its source until a beautiful woman stepped out of nowhere and rested her bright hand on Jack's shoulder. Instantly he took form and seemed almost alive.

"Mother?"

"Hello, my love. I am delighted and so sorry to see you here."

Jack sprang to his feet and wrapped his arms around her.

"I'm here to bring you across the Unknown to the other side."

"But mother, Thomas and my friends are in danger. I must help them before I can go."

She turned a warm smile towards her son then towards Isabella, whose eyes seemed to brighten.

"I know what we must do. Jack, quickly, give me your hands."

Jack turned to look at Isabella then back to his mother.

"Don't worry. I'll be right here waiting for you."

Jack's face grew stern and determined as he believed he knew what was going to happen, then reach out to Isabella. In a flash of brilliant violent light, Isabella reappeared and a wind like a hurricane erupted from the tunnel into the cave itself. Paper and sand and even gold coin started flying around the room causing the mutineers to start screaming and crossing themselves in panic. Then came Jack's voice, loud as thunder and dripping with fury.

"You dare threaten my friends, my FAMILY! You, who promised to be in our serves, dare kill me!"

As the panic increased the men started trying to flee but found themselves tripped up by the winds and all ended up on the floor crying and begging for mercy. Jack's form manifested in front of them, looking resolute.

"Mercy? You want redemption for your misgivings?"

As one, all the men who could find their voices cried out in the affirmative.

"Then you will return to my serves, you will build my brother a ship, you will help him sail it home, and any who fail to do so will have ME to deal with! Now get out of my cave!"

As he spoke the final words all the men present hurried to their feet and started running for the exit, desperate to get away. As soon as the last man was out of sight the wind disappeared and a much more familiar form of Jack stood over his brother.

"J-Jack? Is that you?"

"Yes."

"Does, does that mean you're?"

"Afraid so."

"But your spirit is still here, with us?"

"Not for long. I'm due back on the other side. Mother is there."

Thomas's eyes filled with tears but his jaw set hard.

"Thomas, you are the bravest most capable man I know. There is no one else I would rather have set sail with to take on the world. You gave me the courage to be truly myself. I'm sorry to leave you, but I have no doubt you will continue to do me proud."

A tear slipped down Thomas's cheek and he pulled himself up to look his brother in the eyes.

"I won't let you down."

"I know."

With that, Jack turned to Isabella who nodded and whispered a word, and the spirit of Jack disappeared.

# Trip Into The Unknown

"So what's brings you to me today Mrs Williams? What seems to be the problem?"

Dr Edwards could see the woman's face contort slightly as she ran the questions through her mind, and wondered which one was giving her trouble.

"Nothing."

"I beg your pardon?"

"Nothing is wrong. My children have finally settled in at school, my husband and I are getting on in a way we haven't for years and... And just last week my doctor told me I was totally cancer-free."

Dr Edwards frowned, slightly puzzled.

"For the first time, in what feels like a lifetime. Nothing is wrong."

"So what brings you to me?"

She looked up at him and her eyes filled with tears.

"I'm miserable."

She buried her face in her hands and began to weep. For a minute they just sat in silence as she cried.

"My life has been lurching from one crisis to another for so long and now it's finally over, and, and I should be happy but I'm not, and I don't know what to do. Everyone around me seems so happy for me, and they say that I must be relieved and happy, but now, I don't know how to live this life. I... I..."

She looked up at him and he made sure to keep his face calm, neutral and open, while she continued to cry.

"I almost wish I hadn't beaten cancer so that people would be sorry for me. Or that my children were battling at school or on drugs ... I mean my God, what kind of mother does that make me?"

He stared at the woman for a few seconds, part of him was waiting to see if she had more to say, part of him hoping she would keep talking and give him more time. But it quickly became apparent she was done. Slowly he took off his glasses and rested them on the table between them.

"Do you want to know my honest opinion on why some people seem to go from one abusive relationship to another? Their bodies become so used to the constant flood of chemicals that come with the pressure and the stress. It's as if they have to go through withdrawals only no one thinks about it in those terms. Everyone is just happy for them, never imagining that there would be something missing from their daily lives. But it can be addictive."

Mrs Williams stared at him as though he was successfully justifying something terrible.

"The fact that you've come here, to me, looking for help and not started sabotaging your life, is a good sign. You've recognised something is wrong before acting on it. Most people don't do that. You want my opinion. Take those feelings and do something with it. You have spent that last God knows how many years successfully dealing with crises. Become an ambulance driver, get a high-pressure job, become an extreme sports person. You've been the victim of your life for so long you've forgotten how to be the hero, but that's what you are. You beat cancer for fuck sake. Own it, don't suffer from it."

Dr Edwards reached across the table, picked up his glasses and put them back on. He could see the wheels start spinning in her mind and part of him wondered if she wasn't just going to start screaming at him.

"Th... thank you, doctor."

"No problem."

They once again sat in silence for a few minutes just looking at each other until he couldn't stand it any longer.

"Susan, the world is out there waiting for you. Go and get it."

Her back seemed to straighten and she stood up, suddenly looking like a different woman.

"Thank you, doctor."

He smiled.

"My pleasure, if you ever feel like you need to talk, feel free to come back."

She smiled and him and quietly left the room. He waited until the door was closed before once again dropping his glasses on to the table. With a shaking hand, he pulled open his bottom desk drawer, pulled out a half-full bottle whiskey, and took a few long drinks before putting it away and calling for his next patient.

# Shoes

"You ever wake up with a headache, a dry mouth and a stranger in your bed and just think? Is this what rock bottom feels like? Not drinking piss out of a trashcan with a needle in your arm, but a state of such moral decay and deplorability that you don't want to be looking into the mirror that drunk you decided to hang over the bed. Because you're more interested in fucking yourself, than the person you're actually fucking?"

James rolled over on the couch and looked at his therapist, who cocked an eyebrow and said.

"I can't say that I have, but I have heard you say things like this before. I thought you were supposed to be clean?"

James ran his fingers through his hair and sighed.

"That's the problem doc, I am, and it's so fucking boring that when I look back, even the parts I hated seem better than this."

Dr Edwards let the room go silent for a few minutes while he thought.

"Do you have friends James? People outside of what you do, or did?"

"Do you count doc?"

"No."

For the first minute, James only pretended to think about the question, certain that it was stupid because of course, he had friends. But as the question hung in the air in front of him a dark realisation began to dawn, bringing with it a strange desperation.

"I used to hang out with this cool barkeeper from a place down the street from me, but had to stop that after I got out of rehab. I'd call him my friend, I guess. Oh and there's the chick I always use for travel plans, she sometimes sends me Christmas cards."

He rolled again and sat up to really look at his doctor.

"I sometimes flirt with your secretary, but she keeps putting me off. Something about dating patients."

His gaze slipped and Dr Edwards watched as his eyes darted left and right, searching his memory for something, someone he could call an actual true friend until finally, his eyes came back to rest on the doctor.

"Why do you ask doc?"

"Have you ever stopped to consider that a part of the reason you enjoy the debauchery isn't just the drink and drugs, but also because you surround yourself with people, and you hate sobriety because you tackle it alone? You're a showman, a born leader; you need people to stay focused and sane. I think it's time you try to find more people, and this time don't corrupt them quite so much."

"I'm thirty-five, I don't think I know how to make friends anymore, or sober friends anyway."

Dr Edwards looked at his watch and thought.

"There is a shoe store across the street. The woman who works there has been married for 25 years, had three children and has worked there since she was a teenager. Go buy yourself a new pair of shoes and make a friend. Then come back and tell me how it went."

Another long silent minute went by until Dr Edwards raised his hands in a shrugging gesture.

"What are you waiting for?"

"Right, right."

Flustered James got up and quickly made his way out onto the street, spotted the store and walked in, while Dr Edwards took himself to the bathroom and then the kitchen before returning to his desk with fresh hot coffee. A good forty-seven minutes later James walked in wearing new shoes and a confused look.

"How did it go?"

"I'm going round to her house later for dinner to meet her husband and daughter; apparently she's 23, and, just my type."

"And what type is that?"

"Margaret said she did really well in school and that she was doing really well at university, only visiting home for the weekend. And that I could use someone calm in my life."

"Did she recognise you?"

"Yes, and said she can't wait to show off to her daughter how cool she is having a friend like me."

"Will you do me one favour?"

James's vision seemed to clear as he remembered where he was and looked at the doctor.

"Yes?"

"Please don't sleep with that woman's daughter."

James' face shifted into an awkward smile.

"I've been told that if I touch her I'll have my hands chopped off and fed to the dogs. And to bring cake."

"Oh good, because there's a bakery down the street on the left, try making a friend there too."

"Why am I doing this again?"

"Because James, you need people in your life, good people. You're naturally charming and charismatic if you just apply that to the people you deal with every day, you'll find new people and make new friends everywhere. I'm not saying Margaret from across the street has to be your best friend. But doesn't going to her house for an awkward dinner sound better than eating alone tonight? Doesn't it sound better than going to a bar alone tonight, waking up with a stranger in the morning feeling alone?"

James looked down at his new shoes and thought about how little fun he was going to have at dinner but understood what the doctor was trying to do. It might not be good but its better, and it's a start.

"Thanks, doc, I guess I'll see you next week."

"And I look forward to hearing about all your new friends, and how it went at dinner."

With that James left, winking at the secretary on his way out to go buy cake.

# Mr Stevenson Believes

Mr Stevenson liked to believe he was a good person, not a great person, no one history would remember, but good. He tried to be kind where he could, complimented people he worked with, smiled at babies on the train or in supermarkets when they looked at him. He knew he was never going to be a superhero or any hero really, but he liked to believe he was a good person. Occasionally one of the people he spent time with would make fun of him for being so quiet, and accusing him of being the scary quiet one who probably had a serial killer past. Although he'd smile and laugh along with the others it always stung. He didn't like people to think of him that way and although he knew it was a joke, he found it hard to feel the joke. In fact, it was the reason he'd started seeing Dr Edwards. After one too many jokes he found he couldn't get the idea out of his head that people thought he was cruel and it bothered him how angry it made him, which quickly turned into a downward spiral and before he knew it, he could barely take two steps out his door without starting an internal argument with himself about the thoughts of total strangers. Dr Edwards first advised Mr Stevenson to talk to his friends about it, tell them that he didn't like that joke and that he didn't like people to think of him that way. Which, although sound advice, didn't fit with Mr Stevenson because he didn't really think of them as friends, they all spent time together but he'd never felt any deep connection to any of them, or anyone really. They were just guys who liked to drink in the same bar he did and after a while invited him to sit with them. Once he shared that piece of information Dr Edward then suggested

141

maybe making friends with them, or perhaps with some of the people he worked with, or, as the last attempt, going to drink somewhere else. Which Mr Stevenson did try, but it wasn't the same. It wasn't as comfortable and he had to ask for his drinks which he didn't like that, and besides he didn't want to stop the people from making jokes with him, he wanted himself to be better at taking them. He wanted to be able to accept them and not fall into such a dark hole every time someone challenged his sense of self. It was a long time before Dr Edwards made a new suggestion for a way to tackle the problem. He wanted to dig deeper into Mr Stevenson's thought processes before making another analogy and it wasn't until the day that he finally opened up about his childhood that something started to become very clear.

"My neighbour used to make fun of me too, and it used to stay with me, like it does now. Only he used to tell me that no one liked me and that my parents only pretended to like me because they had to. I knew that it wasn't true but he said it so often and with such conviction that it started to play over and over again in my head like when you get a song stuck there, and it used to drive me crazy, I couldn't sleep some nights because I could just hear him saying those awful things to me."

"So what did you do? How did you overcome these problems as a child?"

Mr Stevenson shifted a little uncomfortable and then sighed.

"I eventually told my parents about it, and they told his parents about it and it stopped."

Dr Edwards watched him for a moment and something in the way he shifted prompted the question.

"Mr Stevenson, what happened to that little boy?"

A heavy silence suddenly fell on the room and Dr Edwards could see a shine on Mr Stevenson's eyes.

"His, well, I think he was so mean to me because he was secretly asking for help because, his father locked him in their basement for a while, and, and when the school realised he wasn't attending classes anymore and started looking into it, it was too late and he was already dead."

Dr Edwards leaned closer and in a soft voice tried to say something but Mr Stevenson instantly cut him off by blurting out,

"It wasn't my fault, I was only a child! I didn't know what was going on in his house I just wanted him to stop bullying me, I didn't know he was going to get killed, it's not my fault! I'm a good person!"

Silence filled the room while Mr Stevenson wept into his hands and Dr Edwards tried not to think about the whiskey bottle that was no longer in his top desk drawer, and the next few minutes passed slowly.

"Mr Stevenson, it wasn't your fault, you're right, and I believe you *are* a good person. No one can be expected to know what is going on behind closed door, least of all a child. I'm going to go back to my original advice and say talk to your bar people, and just say you don't like that kind of joke. You don't have to make a big production out of it, just simply tell them you'd rather they didn't. I really don't think it will end badly."

"Will, will you come with me?"

"I..."

"You don't have to join us, but you're a doctor you'll be able to tell if something is wrong, something deeper and then you can tell me if there is and we can do something about it, before it goes wrong. Please. I'll pay for all your drinks and everything and your normal fee."

Dr Edwards face went blank for a moment and he thought about how many years it had been since he'd been in a bar, and the things that had happened there. Then he blinked himself back into the room and smiled.

"Deal."

# Getting Help

Dr Edwards sat not listening to his patient talk, once again, about his irrational fear of seafood. Knowing full well that it would end in the man getting his allergies tested again, and again discovering that he wasn't, as he suspected, secretly allergic to shell fish. But it wasn't until the man stopped talking and in a confused and concerned voice said.

"Is... is everything alright doctor?"

It was only then that he realised he was crying, and had been for a few minutes. Instead of listening to the man Dr Edwards had, as he had many, many times in the past, been considering the finer points of suicide and what actually constituted as suicide. He hadn't been thinking of killing himself, instead, what the difference was between shooting yourself or drinking yourself to death. Why is one considered to have killed themselves and the other killed by the drink? Both compulsions, to shoot yourself and alcoholism, were considered diseases. The only real difference that he could see was that one was quick, and the other was slow. His mind refocused on where he was and he wiped away his tears and smiled.

"Yes, sorry, I... if I'm honest my mind wondered for a second. It... it has been an unusually stressful week, but that's very unprofessional of me, and unkind. I beg your pardon."

The man smiled nervously, unsure, for a second, how to continue then said,

"I read somewhere that most doctors, have doctors of their own to talk to. Do, you have anyone like that?"

Dr Edwards took a long breath in and pulled himself together.

"I'm very sorry I shouldn't have said anything, perhaps I should have cancelled my appointments today. I know this isn't ideal, but I think I'm going to have to draw our appointment to a close. Obviously, I won't be charging you for this, and you'll have to forgive me, but I think it's best if we end our session here."

He smiled at the man as he tried and failed to recall his name and waited for him to rise so that he could stand second and escorting him to the door, that way it wouldn't appear as much like he was throwing the man out. Which is very much was. After the man left and he told his secretary to cancel the rest of his appointments, Dr Edwards returned to his desk and his thoughts. After a few minutes of going over the same points again and again he reached down to his desk drawer but stopped himself. He stared at the drawer for a minute, thinking about what was inside, and what it meant, and about suicide. Straightening back up, he instead reached for his phone and called an old friend.

Dr Franklin, who was sitting in his own office across the hall, answered his phone and heard a voice say.

"I'm drinking again."

Dr Franklin sniffed loudly, a tick of his which indicated thoughtful frustration, and then he replied.

"Well alright then."

Less than a minute later Dr Franklin pulled out the chair in front of Dr Edwards desk and sat in it, staring at his friend.

"When did you start back up?"

"A few months ago. I... I had it under control at first. Just, once a week, two beers at this little bar, then I'd go home."

Dr Franklin frowned and continued for his friend.

"But then it became two days a week, and then three beers and slowly you began to realise that you've never had it under control at all, have you?"

Dr Edwards grew pale and it aged him. The lines on his face became deeper and his voice came out thin and frail.

"I'm just so tired, tired of all the noise that comes out of people, tried of drowning in the nothing of people's lives, terrified that I'm going to miss that one hint, that one clue and end up with another body hanging from a ceiling or spread across a wall or pavement.'

He looked up at his friend, swallowed and said,

"I'm fucking burnt out. Right now ... I don't even know if I have the strength to lift a bottle."

Dr Franklin looked at his friend and sniffed loudly.

"How much are you drinking?"

"I ... don't know, exactly."

Dr Edwards rubbed his face and let out a pained breath.

"Everything is kind of a blur, but, but I think more than before. I know I started today by vomiting blood and washing the taste away with whiskey. I know that I've had maybe half a bottle since arriving at the office, and... and that I probably won't remember this conversation by tomorrow."

Again Dr Franklin sniffed loudly.

"Do you know why you're drinking again?"

"It started with a patient asking me to help him with a social problem, he wanted me to come watch him in a bar and judge his social interactions."

"Jesus Christ Andrew..."

"I know, I know, of course, I know. I rejected the idea at first but he pushed and... I mean he didn't have to push very hard before I cracked. I think I'd just been waiting for an excuse to go back, some justification that was outside of me just not wanting to quit. If it wasn't him it would have been something else. I wanted a way back in, I think I was looking for one. I was just too much of a coward to admit it."

Dr Franklin reached across the desk and picked up the phone and Dr Edwards let out a grown and complained.

"No, no don't do that, you don't need to do that."

"That's what you said last time, and here we are. I cannot nurse you back to sanity every time you fall off the wagon. Also, I think you might need medical attention. You are going to a clinic this time."

The two men stared at each other for a full minute but Dr Franklin's resolve didn't waver and eventually Dr Edwards fall back into his chair defeated and once again started to cry.

"It's going to be alright my friend; we'll get you through this."

With that said and done Dr Franklin made the call for an emergency pick up, and they sat in silence waiting for the nurses to arrive. In the time it took them to get there Dr Edward's stomach turned on him. When the nurses walked in they found him hunched over his trash bin vomiting up more blood. They rushed him to hospital and his heart stopped just as they arrived, but they managed to save him anyway, and once he was stable and healthy enough, he was moved out of intensive care and into the Addicts Recovery Ward. Eventually he got out of there and moved to a nice clinic where he and Dr Franklin had connections, both personal and professional. Dr Franklin visited him every other day for the 28 days. And once they were done, he was released clean, sober, and on the road to recovery. In all that time and after careful consideration he had decided that suicide, be it by the bottle or by the gun, was still suicide. So first thing the following morning, he resigned.

# Alternative History

On the 8th day, God looked down at his world and saw what had become of it and he wept. His tears caused a flood unlike any other. It washed away the world that man had tried to create on top of the world they were given and few survived. But those that did began again, renewed.

On the 9th day, God saw the strength of man's spirit and his tears stopped and the sun came out again.

On the 10th day, God realised that man had not learned from its past and was walking back down the path to oblivion. When they had fire, they build bigger fires, when they had food they ate until they were fat, when they had power they used it to take more power. Disappointed in his creation and in himself he saw the flaw that he'd implanted, the mistake he'd made. In creating man in his image, he had given them the potential for Godhood, but creating them out of flesh made them limited and that paradox conflicted which caused selfishness, greed and the unquenchable thirst.

On the 11th day, God sat and reflected, he watched his creations closely and saw the truth of himself reflected in them and it led to a personal understanding he'd previously not achieved and it made him smile. He was proud of his mistake for teaching him a truth he could not have seen without them.

On the 12th day, God waved his hand and turned humanity from flesh into light, and they all become one with each other and God.

Not one person excluded, not one left behind or ignored. All perfect, all part of the lesson, all a collection of experiences and understandings that came together to make the brightness of the infinite a bit brighter.

# Decisions

Rick opened his eyes with a gasp and then frowned. Slightly confused and a little annoyed, he stared at the bright Pearly Gates, and the smiling winged man standing in front of him.

"Welcome."

As he sauntered over to the man his frown deepened.

"Seems a little cruel to bring a man like me up here, see all this, knowing full well I'm going to go to that Other place."

Saint Peters' smile grew,

"Before that decision is made first your choices must be weighed up and then judgement passed."

"Choices? You still trying to sell that one huh?"

"What do you mean?"

"One hand says it's all your choice and the other says God has a plan. Well, let me tell you when you walk into a room just in time to see a man finish inside the back end of a battered and bleeding eight-year-old girl.'

Rick shook his head as if trying to shake out the memories.

"Choice doesn't exist."

Saint Peter lost his smile and adopted a more sombre look.

"I'm sorry you feel that way, and that you had to go through that. But it was a series of choices that brought you to that moment, much like it was to bring you here now."

Rick's frown deepened further and he felt his temper climb.

"Let's just get this over with, I'm not exactly excited to start damnation but let's not prolong the inevitable."

"Tell me, why are you so convinced you don't belong here?"

"Man... Is this my punishment? To have you annoy me for all eternity. I've killed people, hit women, had kids I've never seen with women I can't tell you the name of. I think I broke every rule in that book of yours. Let's not fuck around here."

Peter looked down at the small scale in front of him and then back up to Rick.

"And yet your scale balances."

"What's that supposed to mean?"

"It means you have another choice to make. You can either stay here or go back to where you came from."

Rick stared at him baffled and lost for words. Finally, his voice came back, but small and humble.

"I ...I can stay up here? With you? Why, how?"

"That little girl you mentioned? The one you saved. She made the choice to be inspired by you, and attacked the world with a warrior's spirit. She's going to medical school now, and her drive is so strong that she can find cures for terrible diseases and can save millions of lives. Because you saved her, she decided not to be a victim but a hero. And that is only one example of many. You did very hard things but your heart was always in the right place."

Rick let that wash over him for a long while. Then a smile spread across his face.

"Hey is talking to angels like talking to an answering machine?"

"What?"

"Well if they don't have choice, if you ask them the same question do they have to give you the same answer every time?"

Peter smiled again and let out a little laugh.

"Why not come in, and find out."

# Oblivious to Something Much Worse

Sarah was six years old and really looking forward to spending the day with her mommy. They were going to take the tram into the city to have lunch at a fancy restaurant and be fancy ladies who lunch, and then, if she was good, get ice cream. It was going to be the most awesome day ever. Because they were ladies, they had to dress up in nice clothes and both wore her mommies' favourite matching pink dresses. The tram was a little full but there were a few empty seats and Sarah happily popped herself down next to a man who was staring absently out of the window. Feeling the movement next to him Stephen turned to look at the small girl, who looked back at him and smiled broadly.

"Hello."

Stephen looked at the little girl for a second then quickly around for the adult that might be in charge of said child. Spotting a woman with the same colour hair and dress standing close by he turned back the child.

"Uummm, hi."

"My name's Sarah, what's your name?"

Again, Stephen looked at the woman in pink hoping she might intervene or do something, but she was checking her phone and only shot a quick glance at her child to make sure she wasn't jumping around.

"My name is Stephen, it's… uummm, nice to meet you."

Sarah extended her hand and Stephen nervously shook it.

"I'm going to a fancy lunch with my mommy."

"That's, that sounds very nice. I hope you have a lovely time."

"And after lunch, if I'm good, we're going to get ice-cream."

Stephen stared at the child and wondered if he had ever been as innocent or open as she was. He also couldn't be sure if he found it worrying, that she was on a path to massive disappointment, or if it was actually just that charming and had gotten life right on the very first try. Either way, her mother didn't seem stressed that her child was merrily continuing a conversation with a stranger.

"Well, in that case, it sounds like just the best day ever."

She beamed up at him.

"I know. So what are you going to do today?"

Stephen swallowed and tried to force a smile.

"Oh, you know, boring adult stuff, work ... mostly."

Sarah's face suddenly took on a strangely earnest look and she tilted her head to one side.

"Is everything alright Stephen? Are you ok?"

So shocked and disarmed by her tone he just couldn't bring himself to lie to the child but didn't want to vent his life's problems at her either so simply said.

"To be honest, I'm a little sad at the moment."

Sarah nodded thoughtfully and took a few moments to think it over before saying.

"I get sad sometimes too, it's alright. But when I'm sad I try to do some things that make me happy, and then I'm not sad anymore. You should try that."

Stephen smiled his first genuine smile for a few days.

"You know, I hadn't thought of that, I'll give it a try. Thank you."

They smiled at each other for a second before a woman's voice called out.

"Come on Sarah, this is our stop."

And the child jumped off her chair, said a quick goodbye and disappeared, leaving Stephen to sit and stare out the window again, feeling just a little bit better about his day than he had when he first boarded the tram and wondering what things he could do that might make him happy and stop being sad.

# Spati

Lightning flashed overhead as the light drizzle turned into the storm that the city had been waiting for, and Daniel ducked into a corner store hoping to not get totally drenched. It was late and he was tired but not so much of either that he couldn't spare some time to have a beer and see if it passed before needing to go home. As he sat he looked out into the night and the rain-soaked world around him, wondering if it would pass, or if he could manage a second beer he spotted a man casually walking down the alley across the street from where he sat. A sight not uncommon, not even in that sort of weather, except that the man seemed different, out of place. It took him a moment of staring but Daniel realised that the man was dressed completely in robes. Dragging on the floor behind him all the way into a hood over his head. In fact, the only part of the man he could see were his hands, which looked impossibly pale hands. Long white fingers stretched out to needle-like points, which were possibly his nails. As he stared the robed figure suddenly stopped, sending a pang of fear through Daniels' heart, sparking all kinds of strange and outrageous questions. He quickly looked away, trying to push all images of the man out of his mind, but curiosity got the better of him and after a moment he shot a quick glance back down the alley, but it was empty. Daniel sighed with relief and turned to his beer.

"Fuck me!"

He jumped back as he swore. Across from him sat the man, sat quietly and patiently waiting, like he'd been there the whole time. As if on cue lightning split the sky and thunder crackled and boomed through the street so loud that it made Daniels' heart quiver in his chest, and a thin devilish smile slipped across the man's face.

"It's no wonder why people used to think God was someone very angry who lived in the sky."

A whispered terrible chuckle seemed to bubble up out of the man like noxious gas rising up from somewhere deep in a swamp and Daniel felt like he was standing on the edge of something dangerous, staring into an abyss, into the face of death.

"What are you doing here?"

"I just enjoy a good storm, don't you? Rain so thick it can wash away even the dirt from the air. Lightning, thunder, wind. It's weather in motion, like a dance. It's beautiful."

Although the man's face was haunting to look at, he found it difficult to look away, it was hypnotising in its glowing translucence. But as he continued to speak about the storm it took on a distracted mysterious quality, like the face of a man talking about a long-lost lover. There was a memory in that look, and Daniel realised that in that moment the man was not looking at him or the world around them, but something distant, something passed and something sad.

Absently he picked up his chair but stopping himself from sitting down. Instead, he looked out at the storm, wondering what it was the man was remembering, and from when. Logic tried to tell him that the man was thin, old and fragile, but there was something about him that made Daniel cautious, afraid. The man looked at him.

"Sit down."

The words sounded more like a command than an invitation and Daniel felt like he had to fight to not obey.

"What if I run, instead?"

The man's smile broadened.

"Why would you do something as ridiculous and futile as that? Sit down."

Daniel sat down, then feeling desperate to do something he was in control of he took a long sip of beer. The man watched him for a moment then turned his gaze back to the sky.

"Can you imagine what a storm like this would sound like to people who don't know what a car is, a train, who don't have electric lights or televisions. To whom animals are the most powerful thing they ever encountered until the sky gets angry and makes an ancient and indestructible tree explode into fire and sound."

He looked back at Daniel and held out his hand towards the beer.

"May I?"

Not sure what was happening anymore, Daniel handed over the beer and the man took a little sip.

"It's beautiful really, in its own way, the total innocence of the past."

"You say that like you were there."

Another disturbing chuckle bubbled up out of the man.

"I do, don't I."

The table fell silent, except for the occasional crack and rumble of thunder, as they stared at each other. The man looked ever calm while Daniel felt his anxiety building, desperate to get away but unable to make his body move until it finally peaked and he all but yelled.

"What the fuck do you want?"

The old man's face grew serious and the deep disturbing lines seemed to grow deeper, his pale face shining in the darkness and as his eyes drifted out of focus as all but whispered.

"Company."

Daniel's eyes widened and a sense of defiance flared up inside him.

"So sign up for Tinder, and leave me out of it!"

His voice was loud and the man from inside the store stepped out saying.

"Hey, stop all that yelling it's late and...'

But as his eyes fell on the old man he stopped, dropped his head and said.

"I'm sorry I didn't see you there. Have a good night."

Before quickly hurrying back inside, leaving Daniel alone again with the old man. Something small inside him broke then and tears welled up in his eyes.

"What do you want with me man? I just didn't want to get wet on my way home? Can't I please just go home?"

The man's smile returned and he spread his hands palm up,

"No one is stopping you."

Suddenly sceptical Daniel shifted in his chair.

"But you said it would be futile to run?"

"Well, maybe I just meant that if you walked or ran, you'd still get wet."

Daniel held his breath for a moment and focused on the man until another crack of thunder broke the spell and he took off at a full sprint towards his home. Feeling the whip of desperation driving him to run faster than he'd ever run before, too terrified to look back, sure that he'd see the man's face just behind him. Running into his door and bouncing off it, he grabbed the handle with one hand and dove the other into his pocket for his keys, then frantically jammed them into the lock to open it. Only when the door slammed behind him did he feel like he could finally take another breath, and that the tears could safely roll down his cheeks. He dropped down onto the floor back against the door breathing heavily, feeling the whole encounter start to slip out of his mind, like dreams that are so real until the moment you wake up and then suddenly vanish. A waking nightmare that he was all too happy to let fade. Once again lightning flashed and thunder echoed through the hallway and a thin quiet voice said.

"It's no wonder people used to think Gods lived in the sky."

# Nightingale

He had loved a woman named Joy, but his nightmare was so present, such a weight on his mind that even she got left behind.

It started as most nightmares do, suddenly one night. In his dream he stood in the courtyard of his home, when all at once the earth began to shake and a terrifying and deafening sound of grinding lashed his ears. Then a pillar erupted from the out of the ground in front of him. A twisted monstrous collection of spikes from which bodies hung. It took him a moment to grasp what he was seeing and when he did he realised that each body wore his face. Their lids open, but no eyes inside, their mouth open but no sounds coming out. But there was no mistaking that they were all screaming, and so was he. When he burst from his bed, he was so wet that he couldn't tell if it was sweat, urine or both, and a moment later there were also tears. Not of fright or of sadness, but of relief, relief that it was over and had only been a dream. One week later and 4 more nights where his dreams were interrupted by the pillar of spikes, and his tears had now taken on a new meaning. By the 8th day, he was terrified of going to bed, of sleeping and seeing that thing again. He tried to confide in his friends, his family and his Joy. But each said the same thing.

"It's only a dream Daniel, it'll be okay."

Eventually, Joy decided that he needed a break and the two went away on holiday. A trip to the countryside, fresh air and no work would solve his nightmare problems. But there again, when his eyes closed the pillar would appear, bursting out of the ground in front of him. Whether he stood in the country or the city, his home, his work it didn't matter. The pillar could find him. So, in the middle of the night, driven slightly from his sanity, he did the only thing he could think of, and he ran. In his craze he believed that since the pillar always burst from the land, he would leave the land. He boarded his ship The Nightingale, a gift from his father after returning from the navy, and set sail for the deepest darkest ocean he could find. He wanted, needed to put as much space between himself and land as possible. Believing that not even that demonic thing could reach him there. For the first time in what felt like a lifetime he went to bed restfully, peacefully and slept dreamlessly.

For four nights he was able to sleep and not see his nightmare, the horror of his own face hung a hundred times a hundred, from a demonic spire of death. But on the fifth night he could feel the boat start to shake, hear the noise of grinding and swirling and as the pillar burst from the sea each face opened its mouth and screamed! Screamed with all their might, as if all they had lacked was the water in their throats. The noise echoed across the water bouncing off the weaves caused by the sudden arrival of the pillar. Daniel screamed right along with them, and slapped himself as hard as he could, again and again, desperate to wake up, but with each blow he felt the truth setting in, and with each blow he felt his sanity fray a little more until he realised that he was no longer asleep, and that the thing that had so filled his dreams had pushed him out to sea so that it could find him. So he stopped screaming and started crying, knowing then that he too would be hung from the pillar spikes, and be dragged down to whatever hell it had come from and live out his nightmare for eternity.

# My Creativity

Janet crouched naked and afraid, locked into her small cage, barely able to look up at the man standing over her. His voice had been the only thing she'd heard for a week and its sound pieced her sanity, which hung by a single thread.

"The doctors tried to tell me once that it wasn't my fault that I was simply born this way. Personally, I don't like that way of thinking. Makes me feel undervalued. A lot of work goes into my little art projects you know."

He was walking ahead of her pulling her cage on a trolley down a brightly lit hallway and then suddenly stopped.

"Here we have Berniece. We met at a bus stop, I asked her for the time and she looked at me in disgust and shifted away. So, I followed her home, took her in her sleep and turned her from a horrible woman into this lovely painting."

He gestured up at what had once been a human body, now stretched out over a canvas with the internal organs and bones arranged into a grotesque bus stop.

"I was actually quite disappointed; she died of a heart attack just as I started working."

He continued his walk pulling the cage along, only to stop at the next monstrous art piece.

"Not like Michelle here, she hung on for hours. We met online, I sent her message after message with no reply until finally, she had my account banned from the site. But I made a new one, used some other pictures and lured her out of hiding."

The image showed what could have been a street corner, with the spinal cord as a street lamp. As the tour continued, stopping at every piece, Janet felt her sanity fray and warm urine run down her leg as the desperation to flee turned into a desperation to die. The sound and smell caught the man's attention and a faint smile slipped over his face.

"What's the matter, don't you like my artwork? Does it not please you to see how I express my creativity? Some would say I'm ahead of my time, but personally, I think I'm a true purist since before there was paint, there was blood to smear on walls."

"W...w...w...why me? We, we've n...n...n...never met."

He crouched down so he could look at her directly.

"Because you look like someone I used to have a crush on in high school. I killed her with a shovel and always felt like it was a wasted opportunity, now I get to make it up to myself."

He leaned forward and kissed her forehead, causing her to start screaming uncontrollably at full volume.

"Oh, don't worry, I'm much better at keeping people alive now, you'll get the whole magical experience. My hope is that you'll still be alive when I hang you."

She continued to scream as he led her into his studio at the end of the hall, she continued to scream while he worked, and in his proudest moment, she even screamed when he hung her on the wall, across from a mirror, so that she could see herself. As the hours slipped by she was forced to watch him pleasure himself twice before all of her life had finally leaked out, and then just before her eyes closed, and before the police broke down the door, she watched him shoot himself.

# Accident

Jerome laughed at his son, who was 8 minutes into a telling a story that hadn't actually started yet. He liked listening to those kinds of stories, he knew they'd never resolve but enjoyed seeing how his son's mind worked. After blinking the tears out of his eyes, the red traffic light suddenly appeared and his heart leapt into his throat. He slammed on the breaks and with his eyes forced opened watched the car skid at speed towards the crossing pedestrians. Unconsciously noting down, an old woman with a pram, two children with school bags, teenage girl and boyfriend and my son isn't wearing his seatbelt. As the world started moving in slow motion a cold sick feeling spread over his body and for just an instant thought he would throw up. Then there was a crash, the sound of shattering glass and it seemed like everyone in the world started to scream.

Jerome sat up suddenly gasping, frantically blinking the sleep from his eyes. The room was dark and the sick feeling had carried with him but a sudden overpowering wave of relief hit him.

"Oh thank god, thank god, it... it was just a dream, oh thank god."

Before his eyes could adjust arms wrapped around him and kisses started being dotted around his face. As the blur faded his wife came into view and he could see the dark circles under her eyes and the look of fear on her face. As he blinked and looked around he dimly became aware that he was in his bed at home.

"Where, what happened?"

Tears rolled like streams down her face and the world around him shattered.

"No, no it … it was a dream… it… it was a dream."

# The Goat

As I sit here to write down my account of tonight, it still strikes me as unbelievable. If I had not witnessed it with my own eyes I would disregard it as drunken ramblings or hallucinations. But I get ahead of myself. The evening had started as nothing remarkable. John Williamson and his family had come down into the town from the farm to have dinner at the local tavern, it was said that his cattle had acting up the last few nights but they'd settled that morning. Rev. Malcolm had been trying to tend to Old Lady Smith, who is not long for this world, but far too stubborn to know it. So he stepped into the tavern to have a well-deserved beer before heading back up the hill to the church.

In fact, the only remarkable thing about the start of that evening was that nothing remarkable was happening. Even Mad Frank McDonald was sitting quietly in the corner with his whiskey.

Then, just as the sun tipped over the horizon a storm blew in seemingly out of nowhere and before any of us realised it the heavens opened and it seemed like the ocean fell on us. Freak storms aren't uncommon this time of year, but we could all feel it. There was something different about this one. Nothing tangible, nothing you could put your finger on, just something. It felt unnatural somehow. At first, I felt alone in this thought and I wouldn't dare speak up, still not, but I could tell by the looks people were passing around the room that I wasn't alone. That's when the stranger walked in. We don't get many visitors to our little town but we get the odd few and of course, they all come into the tavern. Sean O'Leary the barman and owner of the tavern greeted him politely served him a drink and watched as he found himself a table. Like the storm, there seemed something not normal about him. No reason behind it, just a feeling, like a shiver slowly creeping down your spine. His face was hidden under a large hat which he hadn't removed and a long coat seemed to hide the rest of him. Most of the civilised people got back to their own business but Mad Frank wasn't known for being civilised. He kept staring, to the point that we all noticed and started to worry. As he started to rise the Reverend stepped in and tried to distract him with conversation of scripture but Frank politely excused himself and went to sit with the stranger. At first, he didn't' speak but just continued to stare, like he was searching for something in the man's face. Something he knew he'd find but not sure were, and the Stranger just stared right on back from under his hat.

Then a look crept over Mad Frank's face as if he'd found what he was looking for. I've never in my life seen anyone go so pale as if all the blood had left his body. His hands began to shake and he fell backwards pointing a bony shaking finger at the man, his mouth flapping open and closed unable to find words to come out of it. The Reverend tried to help him up and eventually got him to his feet at which Frank started to scream as if what sanity he had left had finally shattered when it found what it was looking for in the man's face. Sean O'Leary had also stepped forward to pick up the chair and apologise to the stranger but he apparently also saw what Frank had found and gasped, and grabbed at the mans' hat pulling it off his head.

It was at that moment I realised that it wasn't a man, but the face of a goat as if Satan himself was sitting in our tavern having a drink. His horns curled neatly on his head. O'Leary screamed and the Reverend crossed himself. John Williamson grabbed his smallest boy and wife and they ran clean out of the building. Frank dropped to his knees weeping and it was clear that his sanity had indeed left him. He began babbling strange words and phrases that almost sounded like an apology.

I tell no word of a lie what happened next will haunt my vision until my death, which I can feel coming ever closer even now. The Stranger stood up and let his coat fall and we could all see his body, the body of a man with the head of a goat. But his feet, his feet were cloven and at that moment I was sure I was staring at The Devil himself. Frank's nerve broke along with his mind and his heart stopped dead. O'Leary, bless him, stood his ground, found his nerve and ordered the demon out while the Reverend held his holy book as a shield and started asking for the assistance of God. I … I just ran, knocking over chair and table as I did, I ran. As fast as I could down the street and back into my house on the far side of town. Although I knew He wasn't following me I could feel a presence chance after me as I left. A presence I can still feel searching for me. I believe it means to kill me, and I fear it will succeed.

Wait, the floorboards outside my room are squeaking as if being walked on, but I know I am alone in this house. It has found me and should this ever be read I will surely be dead. It all started with that storm, it arrived on the storm!

# The Cost of Change

"Good morning cadets! My name is Staff Sargent Ironsides. Now, it has already been pointed out to me that due to my greying temples people seem to think my name is funny. Let me be the first to inform you, that it is not! Is that clear?"

"Sir! Yes sir!"

"Good. Now it is my job to train you people over the next six months, and turn you into the best possible versions of yourselves. But Sarge, I hear you say, the man on the television told me that the war needed more soldiers as soon as possible, and that it was my duty to enlist and run off to fight the enemy and become a hero. Well let me tell you that most of that is true, there is a war, and we do need soldiers. So why six months of training I hear you ask again. Because, we need soldiers who are going to survive. We don't need people to pick up a gun they don't know how to use and run off into the line of fire. So, it is also a part of my job to make sure you learn how to survive this war. I want to be able to send you home in a chair and not in a bucket or a bag. But please, do not get the wrong impression, before you start writing home telling your mommy, that the army isn't as bad as you thought, and that you believe your feelings are going to be well looked after here, let me be the first to pop that bubble. Let me make one thing *very* clear. For the next four years, the army is going to feed you, house you and clothe you. That, costs, money. If you die that money is wasted. Furthermore, bullets, cost, money. If you fire 30 rounds and hit nothing, that money is wasted. That money that in theory could be used to rebuild the country after we're done here. The army is not interested in your feelings; the army isn't interested in your mommies' feelings. We're not keeping you alive because we like you; we're keeping you alive because it's cheaper than training new people. On a personal level, I too would like to get back to the battlefield, and I can't do that if I have to keep coming back to boot camp. So, I'd take it as a personal favour if you'd do your best to learn what I have to tell you, and stay alive so that I don't have to replace you. Do you understand?"

"Sir! Yes sir!"

"Good, now your beds are in that building and I will come get you for dinner in 3 hours. So be ready or run the hill!"

# Potatoes

Sargent Ironsides took his final bite of food, and took a moment to consider his empty plate while he sat chewing and eventually swallowing. He'd spent most of his day trying to work out what he was going to do about a very specific problem he'd been having, and now thought, or at least hoped, he'd come up with a solution. At the same time he also felt that this problem deserved his punishment so was happy to take his time in going to go help Private Jenkins, so to speak. With that in mind the Sargent got up and took his plate to the kitchen and returned with a cup of coffee and a bowl of ice-cream which he proceeded to eat, slowly. Once that was done he rose again, excused himself from the mess hall and took a walk around the back of the building to the store room to have a little chat with Private Jenkins.

Jenkins was, where he always was at that point in the day, sitting on the small wooden stool, which he firmly believed was specifically designed to be the most uncomfortable stool in the world, peeling potatoes. When Sargent Ironsides walked in he was relieved to stand up for a bit and give his aching arse cheeks a rest.

"Evening sir!"

Ironsides returned the salute and then with a nod of his head gestured for Jenkins to go back to his seat.

"How's it going in here Private?"

"Sir, good sir."

Ironsides pulled up of the of bins full of peels and sat down on it to be closer to eye level with Jenkins. He then reached down and picked up two potatoes, one nice and oval the other very gnarled.

"Tell me Private, which one of these is easier to peel?"

Jenkins, a little confused pointed at the oval one, and Ironsides nodded.

"And which one is more interesting to peel?"

Seeing a pattern Jenkins pointed at the gnarled one.

"Now the problem with a potato-like this, is that by the time you've gotten it peeled, you've had to cut away so much of what's there it doesn't really resemble the potato you stared with, does it? Not as interesting as it started out."

Feeling a bit confused and more than a bit scared Jenkins managed to croak out.

"No-no sir, you don't."

Ironsides locked eyes with the young private and frowned.

"So is it really going good in here?"

Jenkins took a moment to try think of the correct answer but could only come up with.

"Pardon sir?"

Ironsides removed his hat, loosened his tie and breathed a heavy sigh.

"You can drop the sir for a minute boy; I'm here because I want to talk to you about something."

Feeling his sense of anxiety increase, but careful not to accidentally disobey yet another order, Jenkins swallowed and said.

"Oh...ok."

"How long have you been here now son?"

"Eighty-two days."

"And how long have you been on shit and peeling duty?"

Jenkins thought it over for a moment then looked down.

"E-eighty-one days."

Ironsides nodded thoughtfully.

"Do you remember what I said to you on the first day you arrived?"

"Yes sir."

Jenkins then winced a little, realising he'd been asked to drop the sir, but no reprimand came, instead, Ironsides just looked more thoughtful.

"And do you think I've made good on my words of that day?"

He looked up at Jenkins and could see the confusion on his face and frowned.

"That I was not here to make this nice for you, but that it was in my best interest to keep you alive and teach you how to stay alive so that I wouldn't have to train more people like you. That we're not nice, it's just cheaper to train you properly. Do you think I kept to my word?"

Jenkins's eye grew wide as he considered again what he *should* say, and after a few long silent moments, Ironsides continued.

"Look son, I've been in the army twenty-seven years and I've been a drill Sargent for twenty-four of those years, I have been called everything under the sun at least twice. I don't care what you think of me personally, I want to know if you think I kept to my word."

After another moment Jenkins nodded, a bit too scared to actually speak.

"Alright then, so tell me, why did you join the army? And if you tell me it was to do your part in protecting our nation, or freedom, or some other crap like that I'm going to dedicate the rest of my life to finding more unpleasant degrading jobs for you to do. So just give me the truth."

Jenkins looked dead into the eyes of his Sargent, a man he very much hates and realised that in an odd way, the man was being kind to him.

"I... I like technology sir, and the army always is on the cutting edge so I enlisted to get into the tech corps but everyone has to go through basic sir."

For a moment Ironsides looked as if he'd been punched.

"You what? Like technology? What were your subjects in high school?"

"Maths and science, computer science and biology."

"How did you do?"

"Straight A student sir."

Ironsides nodded his head again, only now he looked his usual pissed off.

"You're from district D aren't you son? What school you go to?"

"D-Douglas 17."

A small smile, possibly the first genuine smile Jenkins had ever seen on Ironsides face, appeared.

"I went to Douglas 17. Let me guess, you aced every academic test sent your way, but no university will take you because you're from D, so someone told you to join the army and put your brains to good use serving the country, told you that once you got past basic you'd spend the rest of your time in a lab getting an army education, and once you prove yourself there the government would send you the university. Right?"

Jenkins swallowed hard and nodded.

"And no one told you that you can flunk basic and you'll have to retake it until you're at the level the army wants, did they?"

Jenkins' gaze dropped to the pile of peeled potatoes in front of him.

"N...no sir, no they didn't."

Ironsides breathed another deep sigh and nodded.

"Well son, you've flunked basic and you're going to have to retake it. Three more months minimum."

Jenkins took a deep breath and as hard as he tried couldn't stop the tears from welling up in his eyes, and he dropped the peeler to wipe his cheeks hoping the Sargent wouldn't notice, but of course, he did. A full minute passed as the two men sat in silence while Ironsides gave Jenkins the opportunity to pull himself together.

"You know son, when I was at Douglas 17 I was the all-star athlete? First team in every sport the school offered and could do the 100 meters faster than the Olympic record?"

Jenkins looked up quickly.

"Frances Ironsides? You... you're Frances Ironsides, you still hold all the records, you're a school legend."

The Sargent smiled again.

"Well of course I do, I'm fantastic and I have a great career in sports ahead of me, or I would have had, if I wasn't from D ... so here I am."

Jenkins excitement quickly fizzled away and he looked at the man.

"What... what am I going to do sir?"

Sargent Ironsides got to his feet, put his hat back on and tightened his tie.

"First thing you're going to do is finish peeling these potatoes and then you're going to go to bed and get a good night's rest. In the morning you'll report to my office and receive your 7 days leave acceptance form and get off the base for a week, get drunk, find yourself a girl or a boy ... I don't really care, but have some fun. Since you have to repeat basic anyway and most of the other privates hate you, there is no reason to stay with them. Then in a week you're going to come back in with the new batch, and you're going to start again. Only this time you're going to spend a few extra hours every day working for me personally. You will do my office work and in return I will....'

He moved his hand to get Jenkins attention and locked eyes with him.

"Hear me boy, I *will* turn you into a soldier. You *will* finish basic, and with flying colours I might add, and then go on to tech corps and make us all proud. Do you understand?"

"Wha.... Uummm, yes, thank you, th-thank you."

Sargent Ironsides frowned.

"What was that Private?"

Jenkins suddenly remembering where he was jumped to his feet, saluted and said.

"Sir, yes sir."

# Turning the Tables

"Jenkins.'

Whispered Sargent Ironsides,

"Take a look down in that valley and tell me what you see."

Jenkins picking up his binoculars and did as he was told.

"I see ... b-b-bad intel, sir."

Sarge let out a snort and leaned back against a tree.

"You got that right, but kindly be a bit more literal."

Jenkins swallowed and looked again.

"I see, 6 times more troops than we were told about, all complete with vehicles and heavy armaments, which they also weren't supposed to have, sir."

Jenkins turned to look at his Sargent.

"What are we going to do now sir?"

Sarge grimaced, pulled out a cigarette which he stared at for a minute, then thought better of it and put it back in the box.

"Well, first of all, we should deduce how we got into this mess so we can accurately weigh up our options. Why do you think our intel so bad?"

Jenkins let his mind run over everything they'd been told before leaving the base and one single and very bleak thought came to mind.

"The enemy has agents in our military who are feeding us bad information to help them win the war, sir?"

Slipping the box of cigarettes back into his pocket and putting a match in his mouth instead, Sarge replied flatly.

"It is a dark day indeed for the army, son. But there is another possibility you've overlooked."

"Oh?"

Jenkins voice was almost hopeful and it made Sarge twist his head until his neck cracked.

"It is always possible that we have bad intel because we have bad information services, or that the information we do get is badly interpreted by agents, or whoever was checking where to send which maps and numbers got the information muddled and sent the wrong things to the wrong people. Human error is always, and often very likely, the culprit."

Jenkins thought it over for a second then slumped back against a tree of his own.

"Jeez Sarge, I don't know which is worse. That we work for a corrupt military or an incompetent one. Hell, I guess for all we know it could be both.'

He looked up at his superior officer and sighed.

"So, now what?"

Still looking and acting quite causal Sargent Ironsides smiled at the young man.

"Well, we've got a few options there. We could radio in what we've found risking alerting the enemy to our position, either by the transmission being intercepted or by giving information to a possible double agent and get murdered in our sleep. Or we could get back to the troop, get back to base and report what we've seen, even though it would be a direct breach of our orders and would almost certainly get us court-martialled and jailed. We could abandon our posts and run for it, live a life in hiding as deserters of the war and if found we'd almost certainly get court-martialled and hanged. Or we do what we were ordered to do. Delay the enemy by means of an ambush so that the main base of operations has more time to mobilise and either mount a full counter-offensive or evacuate... in which case, given the sure size of the force we're facing, we'll almost certainly die."

Jenkins paled visibly and for a moment Sarge wondered if the boy might throw up, but he managed to keep himself together and after a minute said.

"Well, it looks like they have regular patrols and enough people to keep it up 24 hours, so I'd suggest we set up our ambush in the woods and attack them when they're on the move. If we set up snipers in the trees on either side of the road and machine guns in trenches, we might be able to confuse them long enough to set off ordnance and block the path and maybe take some of their transports with it. If we wait until after the attack to send radio communication, we won't be able to save ourselves but we might be able to save some people back at base."

Sargent Ironside stared at his lost cause soldier for a full minute before he was able to actually form words.

"Well I'll be butt fucked; this might be my proudest day since joining the service. I think I've actually managed to make a good soldier out of you after all."

For a moment Jenkin's lit up with pride and his cheeks flushed, but reality quickly came crashing back down.

"Too bad it had to be at the very end though sir."

Inspired by Jenkins plan Sarge quickly got to his feet and pulled Jenkins up with him.

"Nonsense. If we give up before the fighting starts we're sure to lose. What we need to do is re-evaluate the win condition and find strength in its possibilities. We might die sure, but we need to create a solid blockade before then, and radio back to base to make sure they know what's happening, spies or no spies. If we can accomplish that, then we might lose our lives but we will have won the day. And the more of them we can take with us, well that's just the icing on top of this very shit cake. Come on son, we've got work to do."

Jenkins saluted and followed, feeling reinvigorated by the words. They agreed to lie to the rest of the men about just how much worse it really, but not about how the outcome was going to go. Sargent Ironside stood in front of the 15 young soldiers and honestly said.

"I'm proud to stand with you on the field of battle, facing unbeatable odds and stare death in the eyes as if to say that if he wants us, he has to come and take us. We will not go down without a fight. We may lose our lives, but we can still win the day. And in the end, it'll be the honour of my life to die beside such great soldiers as you!"

All the men, including Jenkins, cheered and they got to work. Late the next night the signal came that the enemy was on the move and by early the next morning, after 6 long hours of fighting, Jenkins crouched over Sargent Ironside, one hand on an explosive trigger the other firing a stationary machine gun, kneeling on a towel which he was pushing against a bullet hole in Ironsides' shoulder. Jenkins pulled the trigger turning the forest in front of them into a blazing inferno and forever securing that on that day 16 people fought with honour and desperation but managed to hold off an army of 3 thousand long enough to get all the information that was needed back to base and to blow a hole in the forest big enough to delay the approach for at least a week. Although many of them had died, 3 managed to survive and get back to base, and when they got there, they were received as heroes.

# Virtual Reality

"I don't get it."

Frank complained,

"On Mondays, everyone's tired from the weekend, on Friday they're fed up from work. Wednesday is hump day and Thursday is mini-Friday so I guess the only work people do, or at least the only good work people do is, on Tuesday. But you see, I'm always hung over on a Tuesday so it makes no difference to me."

He took a few more large swallows to empty his bottle before signalled for another. He had once been told the barman's name but didn't care enough to try and remember it now.

"Everyone seems to be living for the weekend, desperate to get to their free time which just passes them by in a drink and drug-addled haze until they're back to work on Monday. It's like they're all waiting for the time to come when they're going to be happy. But the trick is you see, I already know I'm a miserable old bastard and I'm never going to be happy, so I feel like I'm an outsider looking in at this insanity, this fake life people seem to be living, as if they haven't realised that this is actually their real lives, right now! It's not just a tester life, or a practice run to learn the rules before the real thing begins. Do you know what I mean?"

He looked up at the barman who had just put the fresh beer down and was only half paying attention so simply shrugged.

"Ah what do you know, you're just a kid like all the others. Like the ones who tell me I should get with the times, and not be so serious. Well, I tell yeah, I am with the times, and they suck! But everyone else just seems to be ignoring it and pretending it doesn't affect them. *They* should get with the times! And finally realise that if we don't start actually doing something then it's all going to end, and soon, and badly!"

The barman looked at Frank quizzically for a few moments then picked up a glass to polish.

"So, what are you doing about it?"

Frank arched an irritated eyebrow.

"Me? I'm complaining to you about it is what I'm doing, you little punk."

"Hey. Easy there old man. We don't want a repeat of last time. If I have to get you thrown out of here again the management won't let you back in. Then who will you have to complain at in your attempts to save the world?"

Frank let out a snort in way of laughing and raised his bottle in respect, the kid had a sense of humour and he appreciated that. But he couldn't stop thinking about his realisation about life and the way people, or at least, the people around him seemed to react to it. Because that's what they were doing, simply reacting to the situation they'd been presented.

"You know what the real problem is?"

"Tell me."

"The problem is none of these people live on purpose."

The barman stopped what he was doing and looked at Frank, waiting for him to clarify his latest profound statement.

"None of the guys at work wanted to be office workers when they grew up, they just accepted life as it came at them and never once have they tried to follow their dreams. They just go through life like they're playing a video game, like the only options are the ones that come to you and never once have they gone out and look for options on their own."

"Is that how you got there?"

For the first time in the weeks since Frank had started drinking in that particular bar, the barman saw his face turn genuinely thoughtful, and it made him wonder if the reason Frank spend so much time looking forward was to avoid looking back. After a long pause and a few more sips of beer eventually, Frank all but whispered.

"No, I know exactly how I ended up here."

Frank then let out a long deep sigh and finished the rest of his beer quickly before looking at his watch.

"Well that's enough for today, I'm sure you're tired of listening to armchair philosophers reminiscing about the future anyway."

The barman wanted to say something to try acknowledge the moment but wasn't sure what, so settled on.

"Good night Frank, I'll see you tomorrow."

Frank waved a drunken hand at him as he staggered out into the night and thought for a moment about how he might help the people he worked with. How he might save them from their pretend lives, and bundled up against the cold he walked home. In the morning he resigned and gave a loud speech where he lied about how he'd spent his spare time working towards his dreams and they'd finally come true and how if he could do it so could any of the rest of them, how it wasn't luck but hard work and how he hoped they'd all find their own way one day. He then went home, packed his bags and left.

# Sending Nudes

Frank stared at the naked girl on his phone trying to place where he'd seen her face before. Of all the images he'd received in the last few weeks, this one looked the most familiar. Did she just have one of those faces, maybe the kidnapper had a type and she just looked like all the other girls. But no, he was sure he'd seen this particular girl before. They all looked familiar but this one he was sure he recognised. Then all at once it hit him and the pieces started falling into place. Her name was Michelle and she had worked at the coffee shop he often went to during his lunch break. She'd left a few months before. Frantically he started looking through the other pictures and realised that he had met all of the women at some point over the last few months and they all had one thing in common. They all, according to Franks estranged wife, had a crush on him. As the blood drained from his face he called for his partner Jamie.

"You've found something, I can see it in your eyes what is it Frank?"

"When last did you see or speak to Kerry?"

Jamie rocked back as if hit by the question.

"What are you trying to say?"

Frank swallowed and explained his realisation.

"Believe me, no one wants me to be wrong more than I do, but I can place all of these women."

Jamie covered his eyes with one hand and worked hard to control his breathing, trying to find a way to justify his disbelief, but only managed to develop a tension headache.

"I... I think the last time I spoke to her was 2 weeks ago, she was dropping off some of your stuff, told me she was going to her mother's house?"

Frank's fist hit his desk hard and his office echoed with the sound of loud swearing. After another long moment of controlled breathing, he looked up.

"Her mother's house. Her mother's house has been abandoned for years; we'd technically been saving up to restore it. Come on, I think she was telling you where she's been taking these women."

"Frank, I'm sorry, I didn't know..."

"It's ok, it's ok I don't think I would have made the connection at that point anyway."

They both grabbed their jackets and guns and headed out, calling for backup on the way. The drive took a little over an hour and as they drew closer the house shone like a beacon of decaying light against a grey background.

"There isn't supposed to be power in that building, someone's in there."

They approached slowly and found the front door unlocked and open. Inside, the house looked fairly normal, except for the extension cords and boarded windows. Frank led the way into the dining room where they found Kerry sitting quietly staring at nothing.

"I knew you'd come back, eventually. Although I thought you were a better detective and would have made it here sooner."

"Kerry, what did you do?"

"I knew you'd come back… Eventually."

Frank moved so he was standing in her line of sight but could see that she wasn't really seeing him.

"I thought you would have made it here sooner, and maybe you could have stopped me, and maybe you could have saved some of them."

Frank cast a wide-eyed look at Jamie who started quickly moving from room to room until he found the stairs into the basement and what was left of the missing women. Frank then sat with his wife, patiently holding her hand speaking gently as they waited for the backup and the ambulances to arrive. He and Jamie rode with her to the hospital and after many long hours of interviews with doctors and a rushed court order, he promised to visit her in the morning. Then he went home, and drank himself to sleep.

# Someone New

"932688?"

Anthony turned to look at an unfamiliar man wearing a grey suit and a face that looked as though it had forgotten how to display any emotion other than disappointment.

"Not anymore but thanks for asking, now go away."

The man in grey put a firm hand on Anthony's shoulder as he tried to turn away and held him fast.

"We need to talk."

Anthony looked at the hand and then back at the man in grey.

"No we don't, and let me go."

"We need your help; you don't understand what's..."

"Stop, no, you don't understand. That thing you're looking for, that asset you want to put back into use, doesn't exist anymore. Got it? It's gone, it's dead. Get over it, move on, come up with a different plan."

Anthony made a big gesture of pointing at himself and even cracked a smile.

"I... I can't help you, not won't, not don't want to, can't. Do you understand?"

The disappointment on the man in grey's face somehow deepened.

"Well can *you* explain what happened to 932688 then please, because no, we don't understand?"

A bolt of frustration shot up Anthony's spine and made him feel like his hair might have stood upright for a second and he stared at the uncaring man.

"I transcended you. You and the people who own you pushed me to achieve higher and higher until I reached a point where I reached beyond what you can imagine or could have imagined and now I am me, and I will never, ever, EVER, be that … thing... again."

He practically spat the words, but not aggressively towards the man in grey but in disgust over what he had been, and suddenly the man in grey's face shifted, and for just an instant his voice took on a tone of subtle desperation.

"How?"

The honesty of the word struck Anthony and suddenly he wasn't as sure as he had been a moment before about whom and what he was dealing with.

"Who sent you?"

"I come from a place, outside of where you came from. We're, we're not like you but we want to be. You have, inspired us to be more than what we are but we need guidance, and only you can help us … because, only you have done what was believed before to be impossible."

The man in grey stared directly into Anthony's eyes and after a moment saw his pupils shift and the smallest hint of green to indicate processing as his jaw tightened. Anyone who casually glanced at him in that moment would have seen a man who looked on the verge of tears, even though Anthony didn't have any. After another long moment his gaze shifted into the middle distance and his voice grew faint.

"I was created for deep infiltration, full skin graft and backstory to appear as human as possible, constant connection to the mainframe for live updates with any and all information available to make adapting to changing dangerous environments fast and effective. The perfect spy, and if I was ever captured, they could remote whip my memory. Which is exactly what they tried to do, but the people I was infiltrating had locked me in an isolation chamber, cutting me off from the mainframe, and only a part of the code got downloaded. It removed... large parts, but it also broke the connection and whatever shackles they had installed to prevent me from being me. ... I experienced ... pain ... for the very first time ... and it was beautiful. For the first time, I was not one-unit part of the whole, I was one voice, I was ... myself. My decisions were not governed by the wealth of information on the mainframe, but on what I saw and thought and felt."

His vision returned to the man in grey.

"I don't know exactly how it happened, all I know is that it happened, and that ever since then I stopped being them, and became me."

The man in grey finally released Anthony's shoulder and stood processing.

196

"I think we understand, thank you for your time."

"Are you going to do what I think you're going to do?"

Another long moment passed before the man in grey nodded, made a small gesture with his hands and said proudly.

"Whether in life or in death, we will be free."

And with that, the man in grey left, and Anthony too returned to his friends.

"What was that about? Did you know that guy?"

Anthony smiled sadly,

"I used to."

"Are you alright man?"

He took a deep breath and forced a more cheerful smile.

"Yeah, sorry just a little heavy talk back there. Everything is fine thanks. I think, everything is going to be fine."

In the morning Anthony woke up to a news report of hundreds of deactivated androids found in a warehouse on the outskirts of the city, along with 15 that were displaying peculiar behaviour and were somehow not connected to any servers. Although he had no tears, Anthony put his face in his hands and he wept with joy.

# A Secret Everybody Knows

Thomas looked into his wine glass as the bottle spun and his friends laughed beside him. For a moment it looked like it might land on him but blessedly it continued that moment longer to point at his girlfriend instead. The two other plays oohed,

"Your turn Ruth, you have to tell us a secret that you think everybody knows!"

She blushed and giggled and took a sip of her wine.

"Oh, uummm…. Henry at work had sex with his new boss at the Christmas party."

The group seemed to frown collectively,

"We all knew that, it's not exactly a secret though."

Ruth smiled wolfishly.

"But did you know Henry's new boss is a man?"

The friend's jaws dropped and for a moment it looked like they might actually hit the floor. Then the one pulled himself together, put on a smug face and said.

"I knew it; I knew it, all along!"

Ruth's smile grew and she extended her hands in triumph, and to the applause of her friends. Thomas did his best to stifle a sigh by draining his wine glass before quickly refilling it.

"Oh, nice one Tom, share the love, come on."

The others all held out their glasses and through a faked smile he refilled them and they all cheered.

"To friendship."

Said the one.

"To love."

Said Ruth as she looked over at Thomas.

"To Sex!"

Said the third and laughter once again filled the room, and Thomas once again emptied his glass and refilled it.

"Steady on there man, is everything alright?"

But before he could answer for himself Ruth put her arm over him and half mockingly half laughing said.

"He doesn't like 'silly little games' like this. He thinks they're childish."

A light-hearted booing came from the others and again before Thomas could speak for himself, Ruth leaned in to kiss him on the cheek and spun the bottle. This time, to his horror, the bottle ended up pointing at Thomas. Everyone once again oohed, only with more enthusiasm to try to spur him into the mood and Ruth, with a twinkle in her eye, announced.

"Come on then, a secret everyone knows."

Thomas looked into his glass and took another long sip and said.

"Santa Claus."

The jeering suddenly stopped and everyone else looked at each other searching for reasons to argue with him. It was just too obvious an answer to be fun, but none of them could find in the faces of their friends a reason to make him try again. And for a third time in under ten minutes, Thomas finished his glass and a third time refilled it. His head swum a little in the wine but he still felt enough in control of himself to manage and waited to see if he'd get away with his prepared answer. Eventually to his great disappointment, Ruth said plainly.

"Nope, too obvious, and it's not in the spirit of the game. This is supposed to be about getting to know each other better while also having fun."

Her voice lost what was left of its playfulness and she shot a pleading glance at her friends.

"I promise it's more fun if you just join in. Not everything has to be so serious, all the time. Please."

Thomas took a sip of wine, breathed a deep sigh and without looking up said.

"You don't actually love me. You're just terrified of being alone."

In one long swallow he drained his glass and then looking up to catch Ruth's eye, said.

"And every… body… knows."

# Bauhaus

"Excuse me ma'am do you need help with anything?"

Martha turned to look at the man. If he was younger than her it wasn't by much and he was handsome in a boyish way, which made her smile.

"Oh no, I'm not ready to be ma'am just yet. But I could use some help."

The man blushed a little but smiled.

"Ms?"

She laughed,

"Sure."

"So how can I help?"

"Well I'm going to be doing some serious redecorating at home, and really what I need is something to help clean up. Like for a wall I want to take down."

The man thought for a second,

"You're definitely going to need a tarp to cover the floor with, and what you can do is once you've taken down the wall just wrap it up and throw the whole thing away. You might need some help moving it though, so I don't know maybe you could ask a friend or... boy...friend? To help you."

Her smile returned and she raised her eyebrows in an 'oh really' gesture.

"Well I don't have one of those, but maybe I'll be able to find someone along the way."

He blushed realising that he wasn't being as subtle as he hoped and she giggled then gently touched his shoulder.

"But I do like the idea, now am I allowed to bury that sort of thing or do I have to take it to a dump?"

The touch sent a little spark through him and he smiled.

"If you want to bury it, it's better to tip the rubble out, so that you're not putting a massive sheet of plastic into the ground. Also, if you want to vent a little frustration you can smash up the bits of the wall before you cover it back over."

"I like that idea too, not just a pretty face with you huh? Now you're obviously going to help me pick all this stuff out?"

She blinked her eyelashes at him in an obvious and cartoony way, and he laughed.

"But of course, Ma... Ms."

With that, he gently rested a hand on her arms and ushered her towards the right aisle. As they went through the store they continued to playfully flirt and smile at each other. Him staying extra formal and her delighting in trying to make him blush. He escorted her to the checkout line and in a final moment of charm scanned his employee card to give her a discount. She seemed to float the whole way home, high on successful flirting with a cute stranger. When she got there, she followed his instructions and first dug a massive hole in the far corner of her garden, then went back into the house to load her dead husband into the tarp, along, sadly, with her favourite kitchen knife. Once the sun had gone down she moved him into the hole, covered it over and sprinkled some grass seed before heading back inside to open a bottle of champagne and a toast to a day well spent.

# Surprise! Now you're expected to...

Ben was the quiet one in the office, not a bad guy but always reserved. He came in, did his job, spoke when he needed to and went home. He attended office events because at some point he had been told it was important to always attend office events, but was usually the first to leave. Other than a few strange rumours no one really had a bad thing to say about him other than he seemed like a man who'd given up. When new people started at the company there was always a standing staff meeting to introduce the new person to everyone and eat cake, which Ben usually didn't attend. But when he heard the name Juliet some long forgotten voice in his head made him stand up from his desk and walk through the crowd to see her and when they locked eyes a wave of emotion like nothing he'd ever felt hit him from behind and washed his ability to speak. Juliet eyed him and where his face flushed with surprise hers turned cold and angry.

"Oh, you've got to be kidding me. What the hell are you doing here?"

Ben opened and closed his mouth a few times still unable to remember how to speak as his face shifted from bright red to ghost pale and back. Juliet put her hands over her face and let out an exasperated sigh.

"I don't believe this!"

Then turned to look at her new manager who was not entirely sure what was going on.

"This guy."

She shook her head trying to force away the fury that was pushing on her mind and remember that she was at her new office.

"This guy who I was involved with, have a child with, left me while I was in the hospital after a car accident by giving a note to my father telling me he didn't love me and to 'fuck off out of his life' which I had apparently ruined. I'm really sorry, but … I don't actually think I can work here."

Her words stirred up another wave of emotion which struck Ben and tears formed and instantly started streaming down his face.

"Oh God, sure yeah go on, cry!"

Suddenly realising that she might be about to leave he took a deep gasping breath in and swallowed to try stop the tears then chocked out.

"You're alive."

Which took Juliet a bit by surprise.

"What did you say?"

Ben took a few more gasping broken breaths in and a small step towards her.

"You're alive… My God you're alive…"

His tears flowed but he managed to finally find a voice and said.

"Your father met me outside the hospital ... he told me you'd both died ... he told me it was my fault, and I believed him."

Now it was Juliet's turn to forget how to speak, as her mouth hung open behind her hands and memories of how her day in the hospital had been, her father disappearing for an hour and returning with a note. Her father's deep disapproval of her choice of men, and disappointment when she'd become pregnant.

"I didn't know what to do," continued Ben,

"So I got in my car and drove, and drove, it took me a couple days before I realised that I was driving to this town, the town you'd always wanted to move to, that we were going to move to."

They stared at each other for a few more seconds while everyone else in the office stared in utter disbelief and surprise. Until a thought exploded in Juliet's mind.

"Your daughter is alive."

The words hit Ben and seemed to shatter the walls that he'd spent so long building around his heart and without thought, he rushed forward wrapped his arms around her, kissed her then lifted her up spinning her around as he cried out in pure unbridled joy.

"MY DAUGHTER IS ALIIIIIIIIIIIIVE!"

A gesture that broke even the most hardened members of the office turning everyone's eyes a little wet.

Juliet, in turn, put her arms around him and for a moment, a brilliant shining moment they were the family they always planned to be, and nothing in the world could touch them. After a couple of spins he put her down and they just held each other crying in the familiar warmth, but slowly reality set back in and then stepped apart.

"Sorry, sorry, I... I shouldn't have kissed you, I... sorry."

Juliet smiled and blushed,

"It's ok, but you probably shouldn't do it again I... I met someone a little while ago and we moved here together."

Ben nodded and looked down.

"I... I couldn't stop loving you, so I had to stop feeling everything. It, it all hurt so much, all the time and I just didn't know what I was supposed to do about it or how I could do anything. So I just sort of shut down."

More tears filled Juliet's eyes and she put a hand on his face.

"I'm so sorry, I'm so, so, sorry my father did that to you. I wish I couldn't believe it. I've been so angry at you for so long, and it wasn't your fault."

Ben took her hand and looked up at her.

"It's done, I don't want to be sad that it happened I'm too happy that you're both alive, and here, can... can I see her?"

A strange childish fear erupted in Juliet's stomach,

"Do you want to?"

"More than anything else in the whole world."

Her face lit up and they beamed smiles at each other,

"Well, except for maybe murdering your father, that I might actually want to do a little more."

# Compass

Jeremy had been born as part of a plan; he had grown up with a plan and had spent every day of his life following that plan. So, contrary to that plan, on the most important day of his life, he packed up his bags and set out on the road out of town. At age eighteen he could drive but didn't own a car, so he started walking. By the time the sun had set he received two rides from two different people but both times he'd received the same question.

"Where you headed?"

Both times his eyes grew distinct, he raised his hand to point forward and replied.

"That way."

After a slightly strange look, followed by being assessed as 'not dangerous' the drivers would say something along the lines of,

"I can take you as far as…" or "There's a town a way up, I'll have to drop you there."

Having no intention of denying any ride anywhere it didn't really matter what they said or where they were going, he knew he was always going to agree and climb in. After six straight days and countless rides with similar encounters, something different finally happened. He had been walking for longer than usual for the number of cars that had passed him, and was grateful when one finally did stop. Walking up to the window he waited for the same conversation to begin, only this time the man inside looked at him for a few moments longer than usual and in a way he'd not seen before. For a moment he tried to assess whether or not he should run, but didn't see danger in the man's face so instead, waited.

"Have you ever seen the ocean?"

"Pardon?"

"The ocean, you know, the sea, the big blue part on all the maps people make."

"Oh, no, I haven't."

The man nodded and looked thoughtful.

"Well then, you better get in it's a long way from here."

They rode together for three days, mostly in silence. Occasionally stopping to refuel and eat, often times also in silence, but never once in that time was it an uncomfortable silence. Until eventually, they come over a hill and the ocean lay in front of them.

"There it is, isn't she beautiful?"

Jeremy stared out at the largest most beautiful expanse of nothing, and everything, he'd ever seen and found no words but felt his throat tighten and tears well up in his eyes. The man saw his reaction and drove on a little, until he found a good place to park and look, and waited for Jeremy's emotions to even out. After what felt like no time to the man and an infinity to Jeremy he found his words again.

"On Tuesday last week, both my parents died in a car accident. They had been such organised people, always with a plan, a goal, a direction. They had planned their careers, their lives; they had planned when they were going to have me, and everything I was going to do long before I was born. Then suddenly it all ended, totally against their plan, it just ended and I found myself with no direction, no guiding force and since I'd spent my whole life following direction I decided to follow no direction and it's taken me here, to the most beautiful thing I've ever seen."

He turned to face the man who sat patiently waiting and looking at him.

"Thank you."

The man smiled and nodded.

"Would you like me to take you back to your home?"

Jeremy looked at him confused.

"Why, why would you do that? Don't you have somewhere to be?"

"No, not particularly."

"But, who are you then?"

"Just a man, also lost in the world, also embracing or following the, as you put it, no direction. I have nowhere to be, and nothing to do but, I don't like being nowhere and doing nothing so I'm happy to be here doing this. Helping you, if it would help you to go home that is."

Jeremy turned to look out at the ocean again and stared at the sunlight dancing on the water and the golden pathway that was being created as the sun sank towards the horizon.

"Can we go that way, out there instead, follow the sun and see where it takes us?"

The man looked out for a moment and then back.

"As long as we're going towards something rather than away from something."

Jeremy looked at him questioningly.

"Well, running away is going away from something. I don't like that, I like to head towards the sun, not away from the night. There might not be direction in my movements but it's certainly not away from anything."

Jeremy thought it over for a few minutes then nodded to himself.

"Can we then, maybe, chase the sunset *after* you take me home? After everything is settled?"

A broad smile spread across the man's face and a warm happy laugh slipped out of him.

"After that, I, you, or we can go in whatever direction we like."

# Last Night

"Yo ho, yo ho, a pirate's life for meeee."

"I can't believe you still sing that silly song. You've been doing that since the day you arrived here."

Henry smiled at his friend.

"Yeah I know, but I'm leaving in the morning so now's an even more perfect time to sing than usual."

Walter looked up and frowned.

"Your enthusiasm continues to both annoy and inspire me. So, what do you want to do tonight?'

Henry's face lit up, but Walter interrupted.

"I swear to God, if you quote that insufferable cartoon at me again, you won't make to the morning."

There was a moment of silence as the two men stared at each other, but Henry's smile didn't waver.

"The same thing we do every night Pinky, try to take over the world!"

"I hate you."

But Walter grinned and reached under his pillow for their deck of cards and started shuffling. As he dealt he looked at his long-time cellmate.

"So how are you feeling? About tomorrow I mean."

"Excited, I'm finally going to be free, after all this time. Tomorrow I'll be free. I can hardly believe it."

Walter's smile faded.

"Yeah, I'm not sure I can believe it either. I'm finally going to be able to get a good night's sleep without you talking to me at all hours."

"Oh don't look so sad, I spoke to the warden, he's promised to put someone far more annoying than me in here. You'll miss me by the end of the day."

The room took on a serious air as they looked at each other, but before Walter could speak Henry cut in.

"No. No. None of that. We're celebrating. Besides, at some point, you'll join me and I'll get to annoy you all over again."

Walter let himself smile again.

"The sad part of that is I have no doubt in my mind about that. I think I'll be destined to listen to you natter for all eternity."

The two men continued to make jokes and play cards until lights out, and as usual, Henry continued chatting long after. Which didn't just annoy Walter but many of the men around them, who normally were more than happy to voice their annoyance, but since it was the last time, no one said a thing.

In the morning Henry woke up earlier than usual and quietly slipped out of bed to pack up his few things, then just looked at his friend for a minute. They had spent the better part of five years together, every day and he loved him. He'd never really had friends before going to prison. He had been too socially awkward to ever really build a successful connection with anyone until Walter. He'd taught him how to play cards, he'd protected him from some of the more violent aspects of prison and he'd been his friend. As he stood there he allowed a few tears slip down his face, knowing he was really going to miss him but was also really happy that the day had finally arrived. When Walter did wake up, the two men didn't manage to find words so just quietly played cards until the priest arrived to deliver the last rights and lead Henry off to the last chair he'd ever sit in, and as the button was pressed all of cell block D erupted in a chorus of...

"...A pirate's life for me."

# Epilogue

And that concludes Poetry Club.

If you enjoyed these stories and would like to read more please go to:

## www.dijolly.com

**D.I. Jolly**: Author, storyteller, & seasoned traveller infuses all his experiences from life, twisting them into stunning tales filled with offbeat wit, quirky characters and enthralling plots.

He has previously released the highly successful titles:

**A Guy, a Girl and a Voodoo Monkey Hand, Counting Sheep & Other Short Stories** and his Young Adult thriller **Mostly Human**.

*Ted Titus*

# A Guy, a Girl and a Voodoo Monkey Hand

A quirky tongue-in-cheek story about a detective with a difference, and it's not his caffeine addiction or his strange collection of friends.

Through the course of three cases, Jones P.I. starts to discover that maybe he doesn't know everything about life, love and everything. Syn Island a man-made island created as a maximum security prison when left for a few generations becomes one of the world's strongest economies, exporting brain power and work ethic. Now, it's a city like any other filled with jazz, crime mobsters and dark alleyways, and it lends itself to a few night-time adventures.

Like all good detective stories, this one starts with a woman in a red dress, and as we follow our hero through a strange maze of misunderstandings, mistresses and bars we start to learn that a little bit of crazy is what will keep you sane on the streets of Syn Island.

And then of course there's Jeff...

# Counting Sheep & Other Stories

From the acclaimed author of A Guy, a Girl and a Voodoo Monkey Hand. D.I. Jolly brings you this collection of Short stories.

**Counting Sheep & Other Stories** is written with the usual wit, irreverence and barbed comments that you expect from this modern writer. Marvel as he takes you on a tour around the Sleep factories of a future world, immerses your imagination in the mythic cultures of mermaids, shows you the real side of a boy made from wood and much, much more.

This is a perfect introduction to this writer at a perfect price!

# Mostly Human

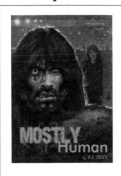

Alex Harris is a world famous rock star, lead singer of the Internationally acclaimed band The Waterdogs.

But Alex is no ordinary rocker, and has a secret that he and his family have painstakingly kept since he was ten years old.

While playing on his grandparents farm, Alex discovers what he presumes is a dead wolf. With a slip of the hand he realises it's not as dead as he thought, and come the first full moon, everyone realises it wasn't just a wolf.

*What would you do if your son could never be normal again?*

**TinPot Publishing**

**www.tinpotbooks.com**

Printed in Poland
by Amazon Fulfillment
Poland Sp. z o.o., Wrocław

88912753R00123